ISBN: 978-1-969842-06-1

For the families we choose,
the warmth we build,
and the light we refuse to surrender.

Quick Word from K before we Begin

Lumenfall is a winter interlude set within **The Eclipsed Series**—a moment of warmth, memory, and reflection shared across different points in the world's history.

Chapters marked **"Long Long Before"** take place approximately **one thousand years before** the events of *Eclipsed*.
Chapters marked **"Long Before"** take place approximately **fourteen years before** the events of *Eclipsed*.

These stories are **canon**.
The events you witness here truly happened to these characters, shaping who they are long before Elara's journey begins. The gods in this world are old, and their pasts stretch far beyond the present story.

That said—this book is meant to be a breather. A holiday pause. A small, gentle moment before things become… considerably less gentle in *Entwined* and the rest of the series. Think of this as warmth before the storm. I promise I'll hurt you properly later.

This book **can be read as a standalone**, and no prior knowledge of *Eclipsed* is required. If you enjoyed this story and want to continue the journey, *Eclipsed* (Book One) is available now, and **Entwined (Book Two)** is available for pre-order.

Thank you for spending Lumenfall here with me.

This book contains scenes involving the loss of caregivers, religious violence, and harm to a child. Reader discretion is advised.

When the Hearth Still Held

Snow had already been falling when Elara woke, the quiet kind that didn't knock or announce itself, only softened the edges of things until the world felt wrapped in wool. The light coming through the small window beside her bed was pale and diffuse, as though the sun itself were still yawning somewhere behind the clouds, and for a moment she lay very still, listening. The house breathed around her: the low crackle of the hearth downstairs, the muffled clatter of a pot lid, her father's voice—warm and amused—cut short by her mother's softer reply. Somewhere closer, Ava made a small snuffling sound in his sleep, one pudgy fist knocking against the wall as if he were arguing with a dream. Elara smiled into her blanket and let herself stay there, suspended between sleep and morning, because she knew what day it was, and days like this were meant to be stretched.

Lumenfall always smelled like bread before anything else. Even before she swung her legs over the edge of her bed and pushed herself upright, Elara could taste it at the back of her throat—warm, yeasty, comforting in a way that made her stomach curl in on itself with anticipation. She dragged her fingers through her hair, which had escaped its braid sometime in the night and now

1

sprang up around her head in wild, coppery coils, and grimaced when one curl snapped back against her cheek. Mira would have something to say about that, she thought, and sure enough, when Elara padded into the shared room, Mira was already awake, sitting primly on her bed with her back straight and her boots half-laced, watching Elara with the narrow-eyed scrutiny of someone who believed it was her solemn duty to enforce order upon the universe.

"You look like you stuck your head in the hearth," Mira said, because she always did, lips pursed in faint disgust. At eight, she was only a year older than Elara but carried herself as though the gap were vast and meaningful. "Mum said you were meant to keep it tied today."

Elara stuck her tongue out at her and ducked before Mira could swat her, laughter bubbling up and out before she could stop it. "It *was* tied. It escaped."

Mira sniffed, unconvinced, and went back to tightening her boots with sharp little tugs that made the leather creak. "Hair doesn't escape. You just don't listen."

Ava chose that moment to wake properly, rolling onto his back and blinking at the ceiling before announcing his presence with a delighted shout. Elara crossed the room in two steps and scooped him up before he could tumble off his bed, his small body warm and heavy against her chest, his curls—paler than hers, sun-bright—flattened on one side. He smelled faintly of sleep and milk and something sweet she couldn't name, and he laughed when she bounced him once, twice, his hands grabbing for her hair with sticky determination.

"Careful," Rowan said from the doorway, already dressed and pulling on his gloves, his voice calm and steady in the way that made Elara feel anchored even when she didn't realize she needed it. At eleven, he moved through the house with a quiet confidence, long-limbed and quick, his hair pulled back out of his face as though he were always on the verge of running somewhere. "He'll pull it all out."

"He won't," Elara said, adjusting Ava on her hip and leaning her head away from his grasping fingers. "Will you?"

Ava gurgled, clearly refusing to commit.

Downstairs, the kitchen was already alive. Heat rolled up the stairwell in gentle waves, carrying with it the smell of bread and simmering broth, and when Elara descended with Ava clutched to her side and Rowan close behind, she felt it wrap around her like a blanket. Kaelen stood at the counter with his sleeves rolled to his elbows, forearms dusted with flour, his skin a shade darker than most of the men in Solia even in winter, his hair pulled back with a strip of cloth as he kneaded dough with practiced ease. He looked up when they entered, eyes crinkling at the corners, and flashed Elara a grin that felt like sunlight breaking through cloud.

"There she is," he said, and reached out to tap the end of her nose with a floury finger before she could dodge. "And my smallest menace."

Ava squealed, delighted, and reached for him immediately. Kaelen lifted him without breaking rhythm, tucking him against his hip as though he'd been born knowing how to balance bread and children at the same time, and Ava promptly grabbed a handful of dough with both fists. Kaelen made a show of gasping in mock horror, clutching his chest. "Betrayed. On Lumenfall, no less."

Serinyá turned from the hearth at that, her expression soft with amusement even as she reached for a cloth to wipe Ava's hands clean. She moved quietly, always, her presence more felt than heard, her skin paler than most in Solia and luminous in the firelight, her hair pinned back neatly at the nape of her neck. When she smiled, it was small but complete, as though it belonged entirely to whoever it was directed at, and when she brushed her fingers over Elara's head to tame a curl that had fallen into her eyes, the touch was cool and steady and grounding in a way Elara had never thought to question.

"Go wash," Serinyá said gently, nodding toward the basin. "Both of you."

Mira darted forward immediately, slipping past Elara to snatch a piece of bread crust from the counter with practiced speed, her eyes bright with triumph. "Too slow."

"Elara," Rowan said, already halfway toward the door, and Elara groaned but laughed, shifting Ava's weight and setting him down just in time to chase after Mira as she darted away, her laughter sharp and victorious. Bread crumbs scattered across the floor, Kaelen called out something about *not running in the house*, and Serinyá shook her head, her smile lingering as she turned back to the hearth. Outside, the snow continued to fall, quiet and steady, settling over Solia and the small sun-elf house at its heart, while inside, warmth gathered and held, and Elara—seven years old, hair a riot of red curls, hands sticky with bread and flour—knew only this: that the day was beginning exactly as it should, full and bright and utterly, unquestioningly safe.

By midmorning the house had settled into the particular rhythm Elara associated only with Lumenfall, the kind that felt both hurried and unhurried at once, as though there were many things to be done but none of them could be rushed without consequence. Snow pressed softly against the windows now, thick enough that the world beyond the glass blurred into a pale suggestion of itself, and inside the kitchen every surface seemed to hum with purpose. The table was cleared and then cluttered again within minutes, bowls appearing where there had been nothing, cloths folded and unfolded, candles laid out in careful rows only to be nudged out of alignment by a careless elbow or a curious child. Elara found herself drifting from one small task to the next, not because anyone had told her to but because the day seemed to pull her along, a current she didn't think to fight.

Serinyá moved through it all like a steady tide, her hands always occupied, her presence calm enough that even Mira's sharp edges dulled in her orbit. She showed Elara how to trim the wicks of the candles without cutting them too short, her fingers guiding Elara's in a light, sure touch that made the work feel important rather than tedious. The wax smelled faintly of honey and herbs, and Elara liked the way it left a soft sheen on her fingertips, as though she'd brushed against something alive. Mira hovered nearby, pretending disinterest while very obviously watching for mistakes, and pounced the moment Elara's scissors slipped.

"You'll ruin it if you do it like that," Mira said, snatching the candle away and inspecting it with exaggerated seriousness. "The flame will sputter."

"It won't," Elara protested, leaning forward to peer at it. "Mum said it's fine."

Mira sniffed, clearly unimpressed with Serinyá's authority when it conflicted with her own. "Mum also said not to touch the bread until supper, and look where that got us." She gestured pointedly toward Ava, who sat on the floor near the hearth gnawing on a heel of crust with fierce concentration, crumbs dotting his cheeks like freckles.

Kaelen laughed from where he was hanging lanterns along the beam near the ceiling, his boots thumping softly as he shifted his weight. "That," he said, "is what happens when you leave bread unattended in a house with a very determined three-year-old."

Ava looked up at the sound of his name, lifted the crust triumphantly, and took another bite. Elara grinned at him and wiped her hands on her skirt, already streaked with flour and wax and something darker she suspected was berry jam from breakfast. Rowan crouched near the door, polishing the glass panes of the lantern he'd been carving the night before, his movements precise and economical, the way he did everything. He glanced up at Elara when she drifted closer, and without a word slid the lantern toward her so she could see it better. The wood was smooth beneath her fingers, the edges carefully rounded, and she felt a small swell of pride on his behalf, even though she knew she'd never say it out loud where Mira could hear.

Outside, someone passed in the street, their voice muffled by snow and distance, and Elara caught a glimpse of other houses through the window—other lights being set out, other families moving through the same motions. Solia always looked different on Lumenfall, quieter somehow, as though the whole village were holding its breath in unison. Even Kaelen seemed to notice it, pausing once with a lantern in his hands to peer out into the white and tug his scarf higher around his neck, his expression sharpening for a brief moment before he turned back with a smile that chased the thought away.

"Cold's settling in," he said lightly. "Good night for it."

"For what?" Elara asked, though she already knew.

"For staying in," Kaelen replied, ruffling her hair and earning himself a glare from Mira when Elara yelped. "For keeping close."

Serinyá hummed softly at the hearth as she stirred the pot, a low, lilting tune Elara had never heard sung anywhere else. It wasn't one of the village songs, and it didn't have words Elara could make out, but it threaded through the room all the same, weaving itself between the clatter of dishes and the crackle of fire until Elara found herself swaying faintly where she stood, the melody settling somewhere deep and familiar in her chest. She didn't question it. She never questioned it. It was simply another part of the day, like snow or bread or the way Lumenfall always made everything feel closer together.

By the time the candles were trimmed and the lanterns hung, Elara's arms ached pleasantly and her hair had escaped its ribbon again, curls springing loose to frame her face no matter how often Serinyá smoothed them back. Mira threatened, not for the first time, to cut one off if Elara didn't sit still, and Rowan intervened with the long-suffering patience of someone used to playing mediator, passing Elara a piece of apple and murmuring something about *keeping the peace*. Ava, bored with bread at last, toddled after Kaelen and tried to copy the way he moved, nearly toppling over in the attempt and dissolving into laughter when Kaelen caught him just in time.

As the light outside began to fade, creeping in early the way it always did in deep winter, Elara felt something settle over the house that went beyond simple busyness. The preparations slowed, not because there was nothing left to do but because it was time to let the day become what it was meant to be. Candles waited unlit on the table. Lanterns glowed faintly with reflected firelight. The snow pressed closer to the windows, and Elara, standing barefoot on the warm stone floor with her family moving around her, felt a quiet certainty take root inside her, small and unshakeable, that Lumenfall was not just something they celebrated, but something that held them in return.

When they came back inside, the warmth felt almost startling, the air heavy with the smell of herbs and simmering broth and something sweet caramelizing near the hearth. Elara stamped her boots and shook snow from her cloak, curls springing loose again despite her best efforts, and Mira made an exaggerated noise of disapproval from where she was perched at the table, lining up candles with fussy precision. Rowan hung their cloaks by the door and nudged Elara toward the basin with his elbow, and she washed her hands obediently, the water biting cold at first and then pleasantly numbing as she scrubbed, watching the skin of her fingers flush pink.

Preparations resumed as though they had never paused, each person slipping back into place without a word. Kaelen had moved on from bread to the stew now, lifting the lid to stir and releasing a cloud of steam that fogged the air and made Ava squeal with delight as it curled around his face. Serinyá laid out the tablecloth—a simple thing, well-worn and patched in places—and smoothed it with careful hands, her movements unhurried, as if the act itself were part of the observance. Elara was set to the task of placing the candles, one at each end of the table and one small one in the center, its holder shaped like a shallow bowl that caught the light even unlit. Mira followed behind her, adjusting each candle by a fraction of an inch and muttering under her breath about symmetry, until Serinyá finally caught her wrist and gave her a look that said *enough* without needing words.

The light outside faded quickly, the sky slipping from pale to indigo to something deeper still, and when Elara glanced toward the window she could see the snow reflecting what little remained of the day, the village reduced to soft shapes and shadows beyond the glass. Lanterns flickered to life one by one along the street, their glow muted by the falling snow, and for a moment Elara felt as though the world were shrinking down to the size of their house, everything else held at bay by cold and dark. She liked that feeling. It made the room feel fuller somehow, as though there were more of them than there truly were.

"Alright," Kaelen said at last, wiping his hands on a cloth and clapping them together softly. "Time."

The word settled over the room, and without being told, everyone stilled. Even Ava seemed to sense it, his fidgeting slowing as Kaelen lifted him and set him carefully in his chair, his small hands gripping the edge of the table. Serinyá took the central candle and held it between her palms for a moment, eyes lowered, and Elara mirrored her without thinking, pressing her own hands together beneath the table, the way she always did. No one spoke. The fire crackled, the snow whispered against the windows, and Elara's heartbeat sounded loud in her ears as she watched Serinyá lean forward and touch flame to wick.

The candle caught slowly, the flame small at first and then steady, and something in Elara's chest loosened at the sight of it. Mira exhaled through her nose, sharp and controlled, but didn't break the silence. Rowan rested a hand briefly on Elara's shoulder, his grip warm and grounding, and Ava clapped once before remembering he wasn't meant to and clapping a hand over his mouth with exaggerated seriousness. Kaelen's mouth twitched, but he said nothing, simply reached to light the remaining candles, one by one, until the table glowed softly, the room bathed in gentle gold.

Only then did the quiet ease, conversation creeping back in like a returning tide. Kaelen ladled stew into bowls, thick and fragrant, steam rising as he passed them down the table, and Serinyá broke the bread with her hands rather than a knife, the crust cracking pleasantly beneath her fingers. Elara took her bowl carefully, heat seeping into her palms, and watched the way the light caught in the curls that had escaped her ribbon again, turning them almost molten in the candle glow. Mira nudged her elbow deliberately and stole a piece of bread when Elara wasn't looking, and Elara retaliated by sticking out her tongue before Rowan could stop her, earning herself a quiet admonishment and a secret smile all at once.

They ate slowly, as they always did on Lumenfall, no one rushing, no one leaving the table until everyone was finished. Kaelen told a story about a lantern he'd dropped into the snow as a boy and insisted had been eaten by a very offended fox, embellishing it more with every telling, and Mira argued with him on principle while Rowan pretended not to listen and then corrected the ending anyway. Ava grew increasingly drowsy, his head dipping toward his bowl until Serinyá intervened and lifted him onto her lap, murmuring something too soft for Elara to hear as she wiped his face clean. Elara leaned back in her chair and let it all wash over her—the warmth, the noise, the way the light seemed to gather around them and hold.

By the time the bowls were cleared and the last crumbs brushed away, Elara's limbs felt heavy, her earlier energy dulled into a pleasant warmth that made it hard to imagine moving again. Kaelen scooped Ava up when he finally surrendered to sleep, his head lolling against Kaelen's shoulder, and carried him toward the back room while Serinyá followed to tuck him in. Mira protested that she wasn't tired, obviously, even as she yawned so wide it made her eyes water, and Rowan laughed quietly and nudged her toward the bench by the hearth where the blankets were already laid out.

Elara lingered at the table a moment longer, watching the candles burn low and steady, the flames unwavering despite the quiet movement around her. She didn't know why the sight made her chest ache faintly, not with sadness but with something fuller, something like the urge to hold on tight. When Serinyá returned, she paused behind Elara and gently tucked a stray curl behind her ear before lighting the final lantern and setting it in the window, its glow soft and constant against the dark beyond.

"Why do we leave that one?" Elara asked, her voice small in the dim.

Serinyá smiled down at her, the candlelight catching in her eyes. "So no one is ever alone," she said, simply.

Elara nodded, satisfied, and allowed Rowan to herd her toward the blankets, her body already sinking into sleep even as the house settled around her. She curled against the warmth of her family, voices murmuring above her, the light in the window shining steadily through the falling snow, and closed her eyes with the quiet certainty that this night, like all the others, would keep them safe until morning.

When they came back inside, the warmth felt almost startling, the air heavy with the smell of herbs and simmering broth and something sweet caramelizing near the hearth. Elara stamped her boots and shook snow from her cloak, curls springing loose again despite her best efforts, and Mira made an exaggerated noise of disapproval from where she was perched at the table, lining up candles with fussy precision. Rowan hung their cloaks by the door and nudged Elara toward the basin with his elbow, and she washed her hands obediently, the water biting cold at first and then pleasantly numbing as she scrubbed, watching the skin of her fingers flush pink.

Preparations resumed as though they had never paused, each person slipping back into place without a word. Kaelen had moved on from bread to the stew now, lifting the lid to stir and releasing a cloud of steam that fogged the air and made Ava squeal with delight as it curled around his face. Serinyá laid out the tablecloth—a simple thing, well-worn and patched in places—and smoothed it with careful hands, her movements unhurried, as if the act itself were part of the observance. Elara was set to the task of placing the candles, one at each end of the table and one small one in the center, its holder shaped like a shallow bowl that caught the light even unlit. Mira followed behind her, adjusting each candle by a fraction of an inch and muttering under her breath about symmetry, until Serinyá finally caught her wrist and gave her a look that said *enough* without needing words.

The light outside faded quickly, the sky slipping from pale to indigo to something deeper still, and when Elara glanced toward the window she could see the snow reflecting what little remained of the day, the village reduced to soft shapes and shadows beyond the glass. Lanterns flickered to life one by one along the street, their glow muted by the falling snow, and for a moment Elara felt as though the world were shrinking down to the size of their house, everything else held at bay by cold and dark. She liked that feeling. It made the room feel fuller somehow, as though there were more of them than there truly were.

"Alright," Kaelen said at last, wiping his hands on a cloth and clapping them together softly. "Time."

The word settled over the room, and without being told, everyone stilled. Even Ava seemed to sense it, his fidgeting slowing as Kaelen lifted him and set him carefully in his chair, his small hands gripping the edge of the table. Serinyá took the central candle and held it between her palms for a moment, eyes lowered, and Elara mirrored her without thinking, pressing her own hands together beneath the table, the way she always did. No one spoke. The fire crackled, the snow whispered against the windows, and Elara's heartbeat sounded loud in her ears as she watched Serinyá lean forward and touch flame to wick.

The candle caught slowly, the flame small at first and then steady, and something in Elara's chest loosened at the sight of it. Mira exhaled through her nose, sharp and controlled, but didn't break the silence. Rowan rested a hand briefly on Elara's shoulder, his grip warm and grounding, and Ava clapped once before remembering he wasn't meant to and clapping a hand over his mouth with exaggerated seriousness. Kaelen's mouth twitched, but he said nothing, simply reached to light the remaining candles, one by one, until the table glowed softly, the room bathed in gentle gold.

Only then did the quiet ease, conversation creeping back in like a returning tide. Kaelen ladled stew into bowls, thick and fragrant, steam rising as he passed them down the table, and Serinyá broke the bread with her hands rather than a knife, the crust cracking pleasantly beneath her fingers. Elara took her bowl carefully, heat seeping into her palms, and watched the way the light caught in the curls that had escaped her ribbon again, turning them almost molten in the candle glow. Mira nudged her elbow deliberately and stole a piece of bread when Elara wasn't looking, and Elara retaliated by sticking out her tongue before Rowan could stop her, earning herself a quiet admonishment and a secret smile all at once.

They ate slowly, as they always did on Lumenfall, no one rushing, no one leaving the table until everyone was finished. Kaelen told a story about a lantern he'd dropped into the snow as a boy and insisted had been eaten by a very offended fox, embellishing it more with every telling, and Mira argued with him on principle while Rowan pretended not to listen and then corrected the ending anyway. Ava grew increasingly drowsy, his head dipping toward his bowl until Serinyá intervened and lifted him onto her lap, murmuring something too soft for Elara to hear as she wiped his face clean. Elara leaned back in her chair and let it all wash over her—the warmth, the noise, the way the light seemed to gather around them and hold.

By the time the bowls were cleared and the last crumbs brushed away, Elara's limbs felt heavy, her earlier energy dulled into a pleasant warmth that made it hard to imagine moving again. Kaelen scooped Ava up when he finally surrendered to sleep, his head lolling against Kaelen's shoulder, and carried him toward the back room while Serinyá followed to tuck him in. Mira protested that she wasn't tired, obviously, even as she yawned so wide it made her eyes water, and Rowan laughed quietly and nudged her toward the bench by the hearth where the blankets were already laid out.

Elara lingered at the table a moment longer, watching the candles burn low and steady, the flames unwavering despite the quiet movement around her. She didn't know why the sight made her chest ache faintly, not with sadness but with something fuller, something like the urge to hold on tight. When Serinyá returned, she paused behind Elara and gently tucked a stray curl behind her ear before lighting the final lantern and setting it in the window, its glow soft and constant against the dark beyond.

"Why do we leave that one?" Elara asked, her voice small in the dim.

Serinyá smiled down at her, the candlelight catching in her eyes. "So no one is ever alone," she said, simply.

Elara nodded, satisfied, and allowed Rowan to herd her toward the blankets, her body already sinking into sleep even as the house settled around her.

The house thinned into quiet the way it always did after Lumenfall supper, sound tapering rather than stopping, warmth settling deeper instead of fading. Ava was the first to surrender properly, his head tipping forward and knocking softly against Kaelen's chest before Kaelen caught him with an easy laugh and lifted him, Ava's arms wrapping around his neck on instinct even as his eyes slid shut. Elara watched them disappear down the narrow hall toward the back room, listening to Kaelen's voice soften into nonsense words meant only for sleepy children, and felt the familiar easing in her chest that came with knowing Ava would be asleep before the night grew too deep.

14

Mira resisted longer, of course, arms crossed and chin lifted even as her eyelids drooped, insisting she was perfectly awake and absolutely not tired. Rowan didn't argue. He never did. He simply waited, steady and patient, until she leaned into him without meaning to, her weight giving her away. He adjusted at once, guiding her toward the beds with quiet inevitability, and Elara followed more slowly, her own limbs heavy now with the pleasant ache of a day spent entirely inside warmth.

Serinyá moved through the dim with practiced care, blowing out candles one by one until only the hearth and the small lantern on the sill remained. The room darkened gently, shadows stretching long and soft along the walls, and Elara lingered near the window as she always did, her attention fixed on the lantern waiting to be lit. She reached for it without asking, already familiar with its weight, the cool of the metal against her palms.

Kaelen paused when he saw her, then nodded once. Serinyá knelt beside Elara and struck the flint, guiding her hands as the wick caught, the lantern blooming slowly into steady light. Together they set it in the window, its glow pressing back against the dark beyond the glass where snow fell thick and soundless, the village reduced to shapes and shadow and other distant lights doing the same.

Elara glanced instinctively toward the back room. "Ava's asleep," she said, more statement than question.

"He always is by now," Kaelen replied lightly. "Still—good thinking."

Mira, already halfway to her bed, twisted around just enough to add, "Because if he gets up and looks, the Lumenkin will think he's lost."

Elara frowned at her. "Only if he breaks the rules," she said at once, because that part mattered. "They don't take children who stay in bed."

Mira shrugged, clearly satisfied either way. "They take the ones they see."

Rowan made a quiet sound of warning, and Mira subsided, though her mouth twitched with the pleasure of having unsettled someone. Elara ignored her, eyes returning to the lantern. The rules were simple. The rules worked. She had known them for as long as she could remember.

Serinyá rested her hand briefly at Elara's back, cool and steady. "The light is enough," she said softly. "They won't mistake him while it burns."

That was all Elara needed. She nodded once and allowed Rowan to guide her toward her bed, the blankets already warm beneath her hands. She slipped beneath them and turned onto her side, arranging herself carefully the way she always did, facing the window. The lantern's glow pressed softly against the glass, unwavering against the fall of snow, and Elara watched it with half-lidded eyes, holding it in place with her attention as if that, too, were part of the keeping.

Somewhere nearby, Ava breathed evenly in his sleep. Mira muttered once and rolled over, the sound more habit than wakefulness. Rowan shifted, the floorboard creaking faintly beneath his weight as he settled, still watchful even in rest. The fire crackled once and then quieted, warmth lingering long after the sound faded.

Elara felt the edges of the day blur at last, the lantern's light smearing gently at the corners of her vision. She held on to it for a moment longer anyway—steady, faithful, exactly where it was meant to be—because the rules said the light stayed, and Elara had never known the rules to fail.

Certain that it would, she closed her eyes.

And wrapped in warmth and belief and the steady presence of her family, Elara slept.

Under a Gentler Moon

Snow didn't fall here the way it fell in sun-elf villages, bright and soft and celebratory; it came down like hush made visible, a slow, persistent whitening that swallowed edges and dulled sound until even the world's sharpest corners seemed tired. Kael woke before anyone called his name because no one ever needed to, not really—his body had learned the rhythm of the house the way a bruise learned where the bone lay beneath it, and it never forgot. The loft smelled of dry hay and old wood and the faint animal warmth that rose from the lower stalls, and the cold pressed close despite the thick blankets, slipping in through cracks with patient familiarity. For a moment he lay still, listening, not for danger, but for the measure of the morning: the goats shifting below, hooves scraping faintly against plank and packed earth; the distant creak of the wind nudging the eaves; the low, steady sigh of the sea somewhere far beyond the fields, unseen and unbothered by snow.

Beside him, Mayli slept tangled in her own blankets like a small nest, her dark hair spread across the pillow, one hand curled around the edge of her cloak as if she feared it might wander off without her. At five she still slept with

18

a softness Kael couldn't remember ever having, her face slack with trust, lashes resting against her cheeks, mouth parted just slightly. Kael watched her for a breath too long, the familiar ache settling beneath his ribs—not envy, not exactly, but something close to it, something that had learned not to ask for a name. He shifted carefully so the boards wouldn't complain, slid from his bed, and moved to tuck the blanket higher over her shoulder where it had slipped. Mayli made a tiny sound and turned her face toward the warmth of the cloth, still asleep, and Kael paused with his hand hovering an instant longer than necessary, then withdrew as though touch itself were a luxury he couldn't afford to waste.

Down below, the goats voiced their impatience with thin, plaintive bleats that rose like needles through the quiet, and Kael exhaled through his nose, already assembling the tasks ahead the way he always did—feed first, water second, check the latch on the north pen where the wind worried it most, collect the eggs if the hens hadn't frozen themselves stupid, then wood, then whatever his father decided mattered today. He dressed quickly, wool and leather, layers built for work rather than comfort, and braided his hair back with practiced hands, fingers moving by memory. In the small mirror hung on a beam, his reflection caught him briefly: moon-elf features, sharp enough to look carved in certain light, eyes too pale this morning, face still boyish in the wrong places, already hardening in others. Fourteen. Old enough to be useful. Old enough to be judged. Old enough to know that in this house, usefulness was the nearest thing to forgiveness.

He climbed down the ladder, boots finding rungs without a sound, and dropped into the lower level where the air was warmer from the animals and the constant press of their breath. The goats crowded the rail when they saw him, hungry and rude, noses nudging, eyes bright and unashamed. He moved among them with quiet efficiency, filling troughs, breaking packed ice in the water bucket with the blunt end of a tool, rubbing one doe's ear absently when she shoved her head into his hip. Her coat was coarse beneath his fingers, her warmth solid and uncomplicated, and for a moment the simple fact of being needed by something that didn't know his birthday or the shape of the sky the night he'd been born made his shoulders loosen by a fraction. He didn't mistake it for comfort. He knew better. But he took it anyway.

Above, the house made its first true sounds: a chair leg scraping softly, the muted clink of a pot, the measured footfalls of someone who walked as though the floor belonged to them. Kael glanced up instinctively. His mother would be awake now, hair pinned precisely, cloak folded neatly even in the kitchen, her hands already smelling of herbs and smoke. She would be speaking to Mayli, because Mayli would wake to gentleness; Mayli would wake to a voice that softened, to a hand that adjusted her collar, to a murmur of endearment that never seemed to reach the loft when Kael was the one breathing there. Kael's father would follow, heavier steps, a quiet authority that filled the room without needing to raise itself, his voice reserved for instruction and praise that belonged, always, to the child he'd wanted.

Kael finished the stalls, washed his hands in cold water that bit at his knuckles, and stepped out into the yard. The snow was thicker now, clinging to fence rails and the sagging roofline of the barn, blanketing the fields until they looked endless and empty. A thin line of smoke rose from the chimney, steady as a heartbeat, and the air smelled of frost and ash and the sharpness of pine. He crossed the yard toward the woodpile, boots crunching, and stacked armfuls of split logs against his chest until his forearms burned, until the cold felt like something he could push against. When he carried the wood inside, heat washed over him and with it the scent of cooking—oats, a little milk, something sweet simmering low for later, because Lumenfall approached and even moon-elf villages, even quiet farms on the edge of nowhere, did not let the longest night pass unmarked.

His mother stood at the counter, back straight, hair dark and sleek, skin the cool shade of moonlight on stone. She turned when he entered, and her gaze met him with the familiar flicker of assessment: what he carried, how he moved, whether he'd done it right. Her expression softened immediately—but not for him. Mayli sat at the table in her nightshirt with her feet swinging, cheeks flushed from sleep, clutching a small cup in both hands as if it were treasure. When Kael's mother leaned to tuck a strand of hair behind Mayli's ear, her fingers were gentle in a way Kael had only ever felt secondhand.

"There you are," his mother said to Mayli, not to Kael, her voice warm as banked coals. "Did you sleep well, little star?"

Mayli beamed, the kind of bright, open expression that made Kael look away before it could do anything worse inside him. "Kael was up," she announced proudly, as if that were proof of something admirable. "I heard him. He didn't wake me. He's quiet."

Kael set the wood by the hearth without comment. His mother's eyes flicked to him again, quick as a knife's glint, and moved away just as quickly. "He should be," she said, tone mild, as if she were speaking of weather. "There's work to do."

His father entered then, stamping snow from his boots, the room shifting subtly to accommodate him. His face was set in its usual lines, handsome in a severe way, his cloak still dusted with white. He paused at the table first, as always, and ruffled Mayli's hair with an uncharacteristically tender hand. "My Mayli," he said, and the words held weight, possession wrapped in affection. "Up already?"

Mayli giggled and reached for him, and he lifted her with ease, settling her on his hip as if her small body belonged there. Kael stood by the hearth, hands still cold, and watched without expression because expression invited commentary, and commentary in this house was never kind unless it was deserved.

His father's gaze finally landed on him. It didn't linger. It didn't need to. "Stalls?"

"Done," Kael said.

"Wood?"

"Stacked."

A pause, just long enough to imply there should have been something missing, something wrong. His father nodded once, satisfied in the way one was satisfied by a tool that hadn't broken. "Good." Then, immediately, to Mayli: "We'll check the lanterns later, hm? You can help me. You're my clever girl."

Mayli's eyes lit, radiant with the joy of being chosen. Kael's mother smiled at her, the kind of smile that made the room softer, and Kael turned his attention to the hearth, adjusting the logs with careful hands so the fire would burn evenly, so the house would stay warm, so nothing could be blamed on him later.

Outside, the snow continued to fall, quiet and relentless, pressing the world toward stillness. Inside, Lumenfall approached like a held breath. And Kael, fourteen and already learning the shape of resentment without ever naming it aloud, moved through the morning the way he always did: useful, silent, and careful not to take up more space than the love in the room allowed.

The morning didn't loosen after breakfast the way it might have in another house; it sharpened into purpose. Kael ate quickly, not because he was hungry—hunger was a constant background thing, manageable—but because the sooner he was finished, the sooner he could move without being watched for mistakes. Mayli took her time, of course, spooning oats into her mouth with careful delight as if each bite were a decision worth savoring, and both of their parents permitted it, smiling when she dribbled milk and laughing when she wrinkled her nose at the heat. Kael watched his mother wipe Mayli's chin with a soft cloth and felt, distantly, the familiar twist of something inside him that he kept quiet and packed down like kindling: not anger, not exactly, because anger required the belief that things could be different. It was closer to resignation, but sharper at the edges. He finished his bowl, rinsed it immediately, and set it away before anyone could tell him to.

"Lanterns," his father said, as if announcing a sacred rite rather than a household task, and Mayli clapped her hands. "Bring them down. All of them. We'll clean the glass and check the wicks."

"Yes," Mayli chirped, and hopped down from her chair, already scampering toward the cupboard where they kept the lanterns for winter, but she was too small to reach the upper shelf and too impatient to wait for help. She jumped once, twice, fingertips grazing wood, then made a sound of frustration that would have earned Kael a sharp look.

Kael moved without thinking, stepping in behind her, reaching up to take the first lantern down. It was heavier than it looked, metal cold, glass filmed faintly with soot from last season. Mayli looked up at him with the uncomplicated trust she gave him, the trust she gave everything that had ever steadied her, and grinned. "You're tall," she said, as if the fact were purely delightful.

Kael's mouth twitched. "You're small," he replied, because he didn't know how to accept sweetness without deflecting it.

Mayli giggled and took the lantern from him, hugging it too tightly, nearly dropping it. Kael steadied it with one hand. His mother's gaze flicked up at the near-clatter, and for a moment Kael braced, already preparing himself for the reprimand that would land on his shoulders for Mayli's mistake, but his mother's expression softened as she reached to help Mayli set it on the table. "Careful, little star," she murmured, and then, without looking at Kael, added, "Bring the rest. And don't bang them."

Kael inclined his head as if he'd been thanked.

They arranged the lanterns in a neat row on the table, Mayli insisting on symmetry, her small hands pushing each one into place with fierce concentration. Kael's father took a cloth and demonstrated, precisely, how to clean the glass: circular motion, no streaks, no haste. Mayli mirrored him with exaggerated seriousness, tongue peeking between her teeth, and when she succeeded—when the glass shone clear—his father praised her warmly enough that Kael felt it like a change in temperature. "Perfect," he said, and kissed the top of her head as though her competence were a gift to him personally. "You've got my hands."

Mayli's eyes shone. Kael kept polishing without pause, fingers moving steadily, cloth squeaking faintly against glass.

It wasn't the work itself that made the room feel tight; Kael didn't mind work. Work was simple. It had rules that made sense. The tightness came from the way every motion was measured, every sound weighed, every breath in the room belonging more to expectation than ease. Even Lumenfall preparations, which the village spoke of with fondness and gentle reverence, took on a different shape here: less celebration than obligation, a performance of devotion to tradition that Kael's parents treated as proof of worth. The last light must burn through the longest night, yes, but in this house it wasn't left as a kindness. It was left because failing to leave it would be unthinkable,

24

because failing to do anything correctly was unthinkable, because everything in Kael's life existed under a quiet, constant pressure to not become the thing his parents already believed he was.

He knew it without anyone saying it outright. They didn't need to. It lived in the way his mother's hands softened only for Mayli, in the way his father's voice warmed only when Mayli answered, in the way his name was used sparingly and always as instruction rather than affection. Kael had been born under the eclipse, and though moon elves spoke of such things with wary superstition rather than sun-elf spectacle, the result was the same: he was a wrongness that had happened to them, a shadow that fell where they didn't want it. Mayli, on the other hand, had come later, bright and perfect and beloved, and the difference between them was carved into the daily rhythm of the house so deeply that Kael had stopped expecting anything else.

By midday, the lanterns were cleaned and refilled, their wicks trimmed to the exact length his father required. The candles were brought out next—thick, pale wax that smelled faintly of pine and winter herbs—and Kael's mother laid them on the table as though laying out tools for surgery. "We do not waste them," she said, and Mayli nodded solemnly as if sworn into an oath. Kael nodded too, though no one was looking for his agreement.

Mayli reached for a candle, fingertips brushing wax, and Kael's mother's hand covered hers at once—not harshly, but firmly, guiding. "Not that one," she said. "That is for the window. The last light."

Mayli's eyes widened. "The Lumenkin one?"

Kael's father's mouth tightened slightly, as if the word itself were childish. He didn't like the Lumenkin talk; Kael had learned that over years of hearing the story told in the village with laughter and unease, only to come home and find it treated as foolishness that encouraged disobedience. Still,

Mayli was five, and five-year-olds lived on stories the way goats lived on hay. He didn't scold her outright. He simply corrected. "We call it the last light," he said. "The lantern is for guidance. Not for nonsense."

Mayli's lip pushed out in a small pout. She glanced toward Kael, as she often did when she wanted a story to stay alive.

Kael kept his hands on the candle he was trimming, careful not to look up too quickly, careful not to invite his father's attention. "It's not nonsense," he said anyway, quiet enough that it could be ignored if his father wished. "It's just... a story. For the night."

His father's gaze slid to him, cool and assessing. "Stories are for children who need to be frightened into behaving," he said, and his tone made it clear he considered that a failing rather than a tool.

Kael's mother, still focused on the candles, murmured, "And Mayli behaves without being frightened."

Mayli sat up straighter, proud. Kael felt his jaw tighten, but he kept his hands steady. He knew that was the point: to make Mayli feel good, to make Kael feel lesser by contrast, all wrapped in the gentle language of parenting. If he pushed, he would be accused of jealousy. If he stayed silent, he would be accused of sullenness. Either way, the shape of the day would not change.

So he chose the path he always chose. He redirected.

"Mayli," he said, and when she looked at him, he softened his voice just enough to keep her attention without making it obvious. "If you want the Lumenkin story, you can tell it to me later. Quietly."

Her eyes brightened at once, as if he'd offered her treasure. She nodded enthusiastically. "I know it," she whispered, conspiratorial. "They walk in the snow and their feet don't leave marks. And if you see them, they take you and you never come back."

Kael felt something cold slide down his spine, not because he believed in the taking—Kael had outgrown fear in the way one outgrew childish shoes—but because he could already imagine his father's reaction if he heard Mayli say it. He glanced up sharply.

His father had heard.

"Enough," his father said, voice clipped. "We do not fill her head with that."

Mayli's face crumpled, confusion and hurt warring with the instinct to obey. Kael spoke before he could stop himself. "It's Lumenfall," he said, and then, immediately regretting the edge in his tone, forced it flatter. "Children talk about it. In the village."

His father's eyes narrowed slightly. "And you are not a child," he said, like a verdict. "Not when it suits you. Not when it allows you to play at superstition. Trim the wicks. Properly."

Kael's fingers tightened around the candle for a heartbeat too long. Wax creaked faintly. He released it, forced his shoulders down, and nodded once. "Yes."

The afternoon continued with the same strained order. Kael fetched more wood. He checked the north pen latch twice. He hauled a bucket of feed, his hands aching under the cold metal handle. The goats jostled him when he entered the stall again, impatient and greedy, and he let the familiar bluntness of their need settle him. Outside, snow piled higher along the fence lines, muffling the world into deeper quiet, and inside, Mayli was taught the "proper" way to place candles, the "proper" way to fold cloth, the "proper" way to speak on Lumenfall night—soft and respectful and grateful. Kael was given no lessons. He was given tasks.

By dusk, everything was ready. Lanterns gleamed. Candles waited unlit in their holders. The house smelled of stew and warm milk and the faint sharpness of pine, and the air felt tight with the weight of a night that mattered, even if no one in this house would ever admit that what they truly wanted was not correctness, but comfort. Kael stood at the hearth with soot on his hands and cold in his bones, watching his mother adjust Mayli's collar with tender fingers, watching his father smile at Mayli as if she were the only good thing the world had ever given him, and felt something settle inside himself with the quiet inevitability of snow: not hope, not fear, but resolve. If Lumenfall required a light left burning through the darkest night, then Kael would make sure it burned—whether his parents cared for him or not, whether the house wanted him or not, whether anyone thanked him or not.

He had learned long ago that some kinds of warmth had to be made.

Kael waited until the house settled into its dusk rhythm before he slipped back out, the way he always did when he needed air and space and a place where his thoughts wouldn't echo off other people's expectations. The snow had thickened while he worked, piling high along the fence rails and softening the shapes of the outbuildings until the farm looked half-buried in white, as though winter itself were trying to tuck it away. He pulled his cloak tighter and crossed to the smaller shed near the far edge of the property, boots crunching softly, careful not to disturb the quiet more than necessary.

Inside, the shed smelled of wood shavings and cold iron, of oil and old work, and Kael closed the door behind him with a practiced slowness, easing it shut until the latch caught without a sound. He struck a spark and lit the small lantern he kept there, its glow weak but sufficient, casting long shadows across the workbench where his tools lay arranged in neat familiarity. He set the lantern aside and rolled his shoulders once, the tension of the day settling differently now that he was alone.

He reached beneath the bench and drew out the piece of wood he'd hidden there days ago, wrapped carefully in cloth to protect it from damp and prying eyes. It was smooth already, worked down to a shape that fit easily in his hands, and he turned it over once before setting it on the bench, fingers resting there for a moment as if steadying himself. He hadn't told anyone about it. He wouldn't. Some things were better made in silence.

Mayli deserved something of her own.

Not something chosen for her because it was correct or instructive or suitably modest, but something that existed simply because she did—because she laughed too loudly and believed too easily and still thought the world was inclined toward kindness if you followed the rules. She believed in the Lumenkin the way other children did, not as something frightening or controlling, but as a promise: that if you were good, if you shared, if you stayed in bed and left the light burning, something gentle would come for you in the night. Kael didn't know if the Lumenkin were real. He had stopped caring about that long ago. What mattered was that Mayli believed they were, and belief, he had learned, was sometimes the only magic that ever arrived.

He picked up his knife and set to work, the blade sliding into the wood with familiar resistance, curls falling away in soft spirals that gathered at his feet. The shape emerged slowly, patiently, each cut deliberate, each line considered. He worked by feel as much as sight, letting his hands guide him where his thoughts could not. Outside, the wind whispered against the shed walls, snow hissing as it shifted, but inside there was only the steady scrape of steel against wood and the quiet beat of Kael's breath.

He didn't think about his parents while he worked. That was another rule he'd learned—some thoughts only made the work harder. Instead, he thought of Mayli's face when she laughed, the way her eyes lit when someone chose her, the way she leaned toward warmth without hesitation. He thought of the lanterns she'd polished so carefully earlier, of her small hands smudged with soot, of the pride she'd worn like a cloak when their father had praised her. She was good. Not in the way their parents measured goodness, but in the simple, unguarded way children sometimes were before the world taught them otherwise.

The knife slowed as Kael refined the edges, smoothing them down so there would be no splinters, no sharp corners to catch small fingers. He tested it with his thumb, then reached for a scrap of cloth to polish the surface until it shone faintly in the lanternlight. It wasn't much—not compared to the gifts Mayli would receive openly in the morning, small and proper things chosen to reinforce lessons and order—but it was something made with care, something that carried intention rather than instruction.

When he was finished, Kael wrapped the little carving back in its cloth and tucked it into the inside pocket of his cloak, close to his chest where the warmth of his body would keep it safe. He blew out the lantern and stood for a moment in the dark, letting his eyes adjust, listening to the muted sounds of the night. The farm felt vast and small all at once, the world narrowed down to the simple certainty of what he meant to do.

He would leave it later, when the house slept and the last light burned low. He would place it where the Lumenkin were meant to come, where Mayli would find it in the morning and believe—without question—that something magical had chosen her, had seen her, had come just for her. Kael didn't need

30

thanks for it. He didn't need recognition. He needed only for her to smile, to carry that belief a little longer, to wake to wonder instead of rules.

That, he decided as he turned back toward the house, was worth any quiet he had to keep, any shadow he had to stand in.

Lumenfall was meant to be magical.

And if magic would not come on its own, Kael would make it.

The Night the Magic Stayed

Elara woke with the uncomfortable certainty that something was wrong—not loud enough to be fear, not sharp enough to be a sound, just a thin thread pulled tight somewhere in her chest. The house was dark in the particular way it only ever was in the deepest part of night, when the fire had sunk low and the world beyond the walls pressed close and indistinct, and for a moment she lay very still, listening. Snow whispered against the window, heavier now than it had been when she'd fallen asleep, and the lantern's glow bled softly through the glass, pale and steady, painting the far wall with a faint square of light.

Her first thought was Ava.

She held her breath and strained to hear him, counting the seconds the way Rowan had taught her when she was smaller and afraid of storms—one, two, three—until at last she caught it: the soft, uneven rhythm of his breathing from the other side of the room, faint but present, rising and falling like it always did when he was deep asleep. Relief loosened her ribs just a little, but not enough to let her settle back down. Something still tugged at her, a sense of wrongness that refused to be ignored, and she shifted beneath the blankets, careful not to make a sound.

The lantern still burned. She could see it clearly from her bed, its light unwavering despite the wind, and that was right—right was good, right meant the rules were being followed—but the house felt different all the same, held too carefully, as though it were waiting. Elara listened again, more intently now, and this time she heard it: a soft sound near the hearth, not a footstep exactly, more like fabric brushing wood, a careful movement meant not to wake anyone. Her heart jumped into her throat.

The Lumenkin.

The word rose unbidden, immediate and sharp, and with it came the rules she had known for as long as she could remember. Stay in bed. Stay still. Don't look. Don't call out. Especially don't call out. Because if they saw you—if they thought you were awake—they would think you were lost, and lost children were taken somewhere warm and quiet where no one else could follow. Elara squeezed her eyes shut and pulled the blanket higher around her shoulders, her pulse loud in her ears as she counted Ava's breaths again, faster this time, as if speed alone could keep him safe.

But the sound came again, closer now, and panic flared hot and immediate, cutting through the fog of sleep. What if Ava had woken? What if he'd climbed out of bed without making a sound, the way he sometimes did when he was dreaming and wanted Mam? What if he'd wandered toward the light, small and unafraid, forgetting the rules the way three-year-olds did? The image seized her—Ava standing at the window, eyes wide and curious, the lantern glowing too brightly for him to understand—and Elara's breath hitched painfully in her chest.

She couldn't let them take him.

The thought landed with the force of certainty, drowning out everything else, and before she could stop herself, Elara pushed the blanket back and swung her legs over the side of her bed. The floor was cold beneath her feet, sharp enough to make her wince, but she didn't pause. She moved slowly, carefully, every step deliberate as she crept toward the doorway, her gaze fixed on the shadowed shape of the hearth. Her heart pounded so hard she was sure it would give her away, and she pressed one hand to her chest as if she could quiet it by force.

She leaned just enough to see.

The hearth glowed faintly, banked low, and the lantern in the window burned steady and true. Ava's small form was still curled beneath his blankets, exactly where it should be, his face turned toward the wall, his breathing deep and even. Elara's knees nearly gave out with relief, and she had just begun to draw back, to scold herself for forgetting the rules, when she saw the movement by the table—slow, careful, unmistakably familiar.

Kaelen knelt on the floor, a bundle of something soft cradled in his hands, and Serinyá stood beside him, her movements quiet as falling snow as she set something small and wrapped beneath the lantern. There was no shimmer, no shadowed figures slipping through the walls, no strange light bending the air. Just her parents, moving with deliberate gentleness, their faces lit by the same warmth that had carried her through the day.

Elara froze, half-hidden in the doorway, the world rearranging itself around that simple, impossible truth.

The Lumenkin weren't there.

And yet—magic was.

She didn't step forward. She didn't speak. She simply stood there, breath shallow, heart racing for an entirely different reason now, as understanding crept in not as disappointment, but as something softer and fuller. The rules hadn't been lies. They had been instructions—passed down quietly, lovingly, so that one day, when you were old enough to worry more about others than yourself, you would know when to break them.

Elara stayed where she was, unseen, watching her parents work with care and intent, and felt something inside her shift, settling into a new shape she didn't yet have words for.

Elara must have made some small sound after all—a breath caught too sharply, the faint scrape of her heel against the floor—because Serinyá's head lifted, her gaze turning unerringly toward the doorway. Their eyes met in the dim, and for one suspended moment Elara felt the old panic rise again, the instinctive certainty that she had done something terribly wrong, that she had broken a rule she could not unbreak. She opened her mouth to apologize without quite knowing what for.

Serinyá only smiled.

It wasn't the smile she wore during the day, warm and distracted, or the gentle one she gave Ava when he was clinging and tired. This was something quieter, more deliberate, a smile that held recognition rather than amusement, and it settled over Elara like a blanket. Serinyá lifted one finger and beckoned, the motion small and unmistakable.

Elara hesitated, every rule she had ever learned pulling her backward even as something new urged her forward. She glanced once more toward Ava's bed, reassured by the steady rise and fall of his chest, then padded across the floor, each step careful, her heart beating so loudly she was certain it would wake the whole house. Kaelen looked up when she reached the edge of the lantern's glow, surprise flickering across his face before easing into something softer, something that made Elara's throat tighten.

"You're awake," he murmured, as if stating a simple fact rather than an accusation.

"I thought–" Elara stopped, uncertain how to finish. *I thought the Lumenkin were here* felt childish now, and *I was scared for Ava* felt too big to say aloud. She settled for the truth that mattered most. "I couldn't hear him."

Kaelen's expression changed then, the teasing edge gone entirely. He nodded once, slow and serious. "That's a good reason," he said, and nothing in his voice suggested otherwise.

Serinyá knelt so they were eye to eye, the lanternlight catching pale gold in her hair. "You did the right thing," she said softly. "You listened first."

Elara swallowed. "I didn't mean to look."

"I know," Serinyá said. She reached out and brushed her thumb gently along Elara's temple, tucking a curl back where it had fallen loose. "And now you know why the rule exists."

Elara glanced toward the small collection of bundles by the lantern, each wrapped carefully, placed with intention. "So... the Lumenkin," she began, then faltered.

Kaelen chuckled under his breath, quiet enough not to carry. "Someone has to be them," he said simply.

Elara considered that, her mind racing in the way it always did when something new rearranged itself inside her. The story hadn't been a lie. It had been a promise—just not in the way she'd imagined. "You make it," she said slowly. "For us."

"For Ava," Serinyá corrected gently. "And for Mira. And for you, once." Her eyes softened. "And now, for them."

Something warm and fierce bloomed in Elara's chest at that, pride tangled with a sense of gravity she had never felt before. This wasn't a secret meant to be kept forever. It was a responsibility, passed carefully from hand to hand.

Serinyá rose and gestured toward the bundles. "Would you like to help?"

Elara nodded immediately, the movement decisive. She knelt beside the lantern, careful not to block its light, and scanned the small offerings laid out there. One bundle caught her eye at once—wrapped in blue cloth, the knot tied too neatly, the sort of thing Mira would pretend not to care about while watching everyone else open their gifts first. Elara reached for it and hesitated, glancing up for permission.

"For Mira?" she asked.

Serinyá's smile deepened. "For Mira," she agreed.

Elara lifted the gift and placed it carefully beneath the lantern, adjusting it so it sat just so, visible but not obvious, the way Mira liked things even when she insisted she didn't. Her hands trembled slightly as she did it, not with fear, but with the weight of the moment. When she was finished, she leaned back on her heels and looked at it, satisfaction settling in her chest like a quiet click into place.

Kaelen nodded once, approval clear. "Looks like the Lumenkin have good taste this year."

Elara smiled despite herself, a small, conspiratorial thing. "They always do."

Serinyá smoothed Elara's curls once more, her touch lingering just long enough to be felt. "That's enough for tonight," she said softly. "The rest belongs to morning."

Elara stood and allowed herself to be guided back toward her bed, her steps lighter now, her fear gone entirely. She slipped beneath the blankets and turned onto her side, facing the window as she always did. The lantern still burned, steady and faithful, the gifts waiting patiently beneath it.

This time, when Elara closed her eyes, it wasn't with blind belief—but with understanding.

And that felt even warmer.

Morning came quietly, pale light slipping through the window as if unsure whether it was welcome yet. The lantern had gone cold sometime in the night, its glow replaced by the thin wash of winter dawn, and Elara woke with the strange, steady calm of someone who had gone to sleep knowing a secret and woken still holding it. The house was already stirring—Ava's voice, bright and insistent, carrying from the back room as he demanded to know *now*, immediately, whether it was time.

Elara stayed where she was in her bed, watching as Mira padded into the main room, hair wild, expression carefully unimpressed. She stopped short when she saw the hearth, the small cluster of gifts waiting beneath the window, and for a heartbeat her practiced indifference slipped. Elara saw it—

the flicker of surprise, the sharp, pleased intake of breath Mira tried and failed to hide—before Mira masked it again, glancing over her shoulder as if daring anyone to comment.

"Looks like the Lumenkin remembered," Rowan said mildly.

Mira snorted, but her hands were already reaching, fingers hovering over the blue-wrapped bundle before she caught herself and pretended to consider something else instead. Elara smiled into her blanket, warmth blooming low and sure in her chest as Mira finally took it, turning it over with exaggerated scrutiny before her mouth curved despite herself.

Elara didn't move. She didn't speak. She didn't need to.

The magic was working.

And that was enough.

What We Make for the Ones We Love

Kael – Long Long Before

Night came without ceremony on the farm, the way it always did—light thinning, color draining, the world settling into shades of blue and gray long before the sky fully surrendered to dark. Kael didn't mark the hour. He never did. There were still things that needed doing, and the day did not end simply because it was Lumenfall.

He pulled his cloak tighter and crossed the yard once more, boots crunching through snow that had crusted and softened again beneath fresh fall. The goats stirred when they heard him, hooves shifting, breath fogging the air as they pressed close to the rails. He moved among them with the same steady rhythm he'd kept since he was old enough to be useful, checking each latch by touch, reinforcing the north pen again despite having fixed it twice already. The wind worried it more on nights like this, slipping fingers into gaps and testing weak points, and Kael had learned the cost of assuming once was enough.

He refilled the feed troughs even though they were not empty, topped the water despite the ache in his hands from breaking ice earlier, and ran his palm along the fence line until he found the place where the wood had begun to splinter. He wedged a temporary brace into place, marked it in his head for repair tomorrow, and moved on. The animals trusted routine. They trusted presence. Kael trusted those things too.

By the time he finished, his shoulders burned and the cold had worked its way deep into his joints, familiar and persistent. He welcomed it. Pain was grounding. Pain meant something had been done.

The house was quiet when he went back inside, the kind of quiet that meant it had already decided it did not require him further. His parents' door was closed. The lamps had been turned low. Mayli's breathing drifted faintly from the loft, soft and even, the sound of sleep that had not yet learned to brace itself against disappointment. Kael paused at the foot of the ladder and listened until he could match the rhythm of it, until he knew she was truly asleep, before allowing himself to move again.

He banked the hearth carefully, coaxing the embers into a steady, lasting glow rather than letting them die down too quickly. The house liked consistency. His parents liked it too. Too much heat was wasteful. Too little was negligence. Kael adjusted the logs until the fire sat exactly between the two, then wiped his hands on a cloth and stood for a moment, taking in the room.

It looked the way it always did on Lumenfall night. Lantern cleaned and waiting by the window. Candles set out but unlit. Everything orderly. Everything correct. If anyone had asked, Kael would have said it was nice. He had learned the value of that word early—*nice* meant acceptable, meant unobjectionable, meant no one would ask you to change.

He didn't remember a Lumenfall when this hadn't been his role.

There had been other nights, other winters, where he'd been younger and clumsier and more likely to earn a sharp word for doing something wrong, but the shape of it had always been the same. He worked. He watched. He stayed awake longer than he should have. Mayli woke happy. His parents nodded approvingly at a night gone smoothly, and the world moved on. Kael did not resent it. Resentment required energy he had learned to conserve.

He crossed to the window and checked the lantern, trimming the wick just enough to ensure it would burn evenly through the night. The glass reflected his face faintly, distorted by soot and light, and he turned away before the reflection could hold his attention. The lantern was not for him. It never had been.

Only when everything else was settled did he reach into the inside pocket of his cloak.

The small bundle rested there, warm from his body, wrapped in cloth worn thin at the edges. Kael did not unwrap it yet. He held it for a moment instead, fingers curling around its shape, grounding himself in the quiet certainty of it. He had worked on it in stolen moments over the past week— after chores, before sleep, in the shed where no one asked questions—and each cut had been deliberate. No wasted motion. No excess.

Mayli would like it.

That was not a hope. It was a conclusion drawn from observation, from knowing her the way he knew the land and the animals and the weather's moods. She liked things that fit in her hands. Things that invited stories. Things that felt chosen rather than assigned. She believed in the Lumenkin not because they were frightening, but because they were kind, because they noticed good children and brought them something made just for them.

Mayli was a good child.

Kael glanced toward the loft again, reassured by the steady sound of her sleep, and then toward his parents' door, still closed, still silent. They would not wake. They never did on nights like this. Lumenfall, for them, was about order maintained and rules upheld, not about wonder. Wonder was messy. Wonder asked questions.

Kael stepped carefully, placing his feet where the boards would not creak, moving through the room with the same precision the village stories attributed to the Lumenkin themselves. Slow. Quiet. Intent on leaving nothing behind but the result. He paused near the hearth, measuring distance and placement in his mind, already knowing where the gift would go when the time came—but not yet. Not until everything was right.

He checked the lantern once more. Checked the window latch. Listened again for Mayli's breathing.

Only then did he allow himself to begin.

Kael waited another full minute before moving, counting Mayli's breaths in his head the way he always did when something mattered. In. Out. In. Out. When the rhythm didn't change, when sleep held her fast and kind, he finally loosened his grip on the bundle and drew it free.

He unwrapped it slowly, careful not to let the cloth whisper. The small carving rested in his palm, smooth and warm, shaped to fit a child's hands just so. He turned it once, checking for flaws by touch alone, then closed his fingers around it again. This was the part he did not rush. This was the part that mattered.

He crossed the room on the balls of his feet, moving as the stories said the Lumenkin did—softly, deliberately, as if the night itself might take offense if he were careless. He knelt near the hearth, the banked embers throwing just enough light to see by, and paused there, head bowed slightly, shoulders tense with the weight of attention. For a heartbeat, he listened for any change in the house: a shift of blankets, a sigh, the creak of a board upstairs.

Nothing.

Kael exhaled slowly and, without quite meaning to, let the words form in his mind.

Mēnó, he thought, the name old and heavy and familiar in a way nothing else was. He did not dress it up. He did not ask for favors or mercy or understanding. *Please. Just let her sleep. I'll do the rest.*

He didn't wait for an answer. Waiting implied expectation, and Kael had learned better than that. He placed the carving carefully beneath the lantern, adjusting it once, then again, until it sat exactly where Mayli's eyes would land first—close enough to the light to catch it, far enough back to feel intentional rather than staged. He stepped away, assessed it from a distance, then nudged it a fraction to the left.

Perfect.

He retreated the way he had come, every movement precise, and rewrapped the cloth around nothing at all before tucking it back into his pocket out of habit. The room felt unchanged, and yet something in it had shifted, subtle as a held breath finally released. Kael straightened slowly and turned his attention outward, toward the window and the falling snow beyond it.

He did not go to bed.

Instead, he pulled a stool closer to the wall beneath the loft and sat, folding his arms against the cold, positioning himself where he could hear

Mayli breathe and see the lantern's glow without having to move. The night stretched. Snow thickened, the world beyond the glass dissolving into white and shadow. The house creaked softly as it settled, the sound familiar enough to be comforting, and Kael remained where he was, eyes half-lidded, body still, mind alert.

If Mayli stirred, he would hear it.
If the fire faltered, he would know.
If the lantern dimmed, he would fix it.

That was part of the work too.

Time passed in pieces rather than hours. Kael let his thoughts drift only as far as necessary, never backward, never forward. There would be a morning. There always was. When it came, Mayli would wake with wonder bright in her face, and his parents would smile and speak of tradition and the Lumenkin and the importance of a well-kept house. Kael would stand where he was meant to stand and say nothing, because saying nothing preserved the shape of things, and the shape of things mattered more than credit ever could.

Outside, the snow erased everything it touched.

Inside, the light held.

Kael stayed awake until the gray edge of dawn pressed faintly against the window, until the lantern burned low but steady, until Mayli shifted in her sleep and sighed, content and untroubled. Only then did he allow his eyes to close for a moment, not in rest, but in completion.

The magic had been made.

Morning, as It Should Be

Elara – Long Before

Elara woke before anyone called her name.

The light in the room was different from the day before—paler, thinner, as if morning had crept in carefully, unsure whether it was welcome. Snow pressed close to the window, high enough now that it softened the edges of the world, and for a moment Elara lay still beneath her blankets, listening. The house felt full in a way she had never noticed before, not with sound, but with anticipation, like a breath being held.

She smiled into her pillow.

Ava was already awake. She could hear it in the way his feet thumped unevenly against the floor, in the rising pitch of his voice as he demanded answers to questions no one had asked yet. "Mum," he called, insistent and bright. "Mum, is it *now*?"

Elara pushed herself upright and swung her legs out of bed, the floor cold but familiar beneath her feet. She dressed quickly, hands moving with quiet excitement, and stepped into the main room just as Ava barreled toward the hearth, his hair wild, his eyes wide. He skidded to a stop when he saw the space beneath the window, breath catching sharply in his chest.

"They came," he whispered.

The gifts sat where they should—carefully placed, small and thoughtful, the lantern cold now but still standing guard above them. Elara felt the now-familiar warmth bloom low in her chest, pride threaded through it like gold. She stayed where she was, leaning lightly against the doorframe, watching.

Mira followed more slowly, her expression carefully arranged into practiced indifference. She made it three steps into the room before she stopped short, eyes flicking to the hearth despite herself. For a heartbeat, Elara saw the real reaction—the surprise, the delight Mira would never admit to—and then Mira caught herself, lifting her chin.

"Huh," she said, as if she had expected nothing less. "Took them long enough."

Rowan laughed quietly from behind her, the sound soft with sleep. "Looks like you were remembered."

Mira shot him a look, but her hands were already reaching, fingers hovering over the blue-wrapped bundle before she pulled them back, pretending to consider the others instead. Elara watched her closely now, heart thrumming with a secret pleasure she didn't quite understand yet. She knew which one Mira would choose. She knew because she had placed it there herself.

Serinyá entered the room then, her steps unhurried, Kaelen just behind her, both watching the children with the careful attention of people who understood exactly what was happening and why it mattered. Ava reached for his gift without hesitation, tearing into it with delight, laughter bubbling up as something small and bright emerged from its wrappings. Mira held out longer, stubborn to the end, before finally snatching up the blue cloth and untying it with quick, efficient fingers.

She froze.

Just for a second.

Elara saw it—the way Mira's shoulders eased, the way her mouth softened before she could stop it. Mira turned the gift over in her hands, inspecting it with exaggerated seriousness, but she didn't put it down. She didn't pretend she didn't like it. She held it close instead, as if testing whether it would stay.

Elara looked away then, heat blooming behind her eyes, satisfied in a way she had never felt before. This was better than opening her own gift. This was different. Heavier. Like stepping into shoes she hadn't known were waiting for her.

Kaelen caught her eye across the room and gave her a look that made her straighten just a little, pride and something like understanding passing between them without words. Serinyá's smile was softer still, knowing and warm.

Lumenfall, Elara realized, wasn't just about what you received.

It was about what you carried forward.

She turned back to the window, to the snow beyond it and the lantern that had burned through the night and felt the truth of it settle deep and sure inside her. The magic hadn't gone anywhere. It had simply changed hands.

And Elara was ready to hold it.

Elara lingered by the window a moment longer than she needed to, watching the snow fall thick and quiet beyond the glass. The room behind her was full of sound now—Ava's laughter, Rowan's voice, Mira pretending she didn't care while caring very much—and Elara held it all close, afraid that if she breathed too deeply it might scatter.

She wished, suddenly and fiercely, that it could always feel like this. That every Lumenfall would be warm and full and certain.
That the magic would never change hands again.

The thought had barely settled when the world seemed to tilt—not sharply, not frighteningly, just enough that her vision blurred at the edges. For the briefest heartbeat, the hearth before her was not the one she knew.

It was larger. Richer. Draped in Lumenfall greenery and light, the fire burning high and bright. Two men stood before it, laughing as they moved— one with long, dark hair falling loose down his back, his presence deep and shadowed even in joy; the other fairer, medium-blond hair catching the firelight as he crouched to scoop up a pair of small, identical children who shrieked with delight. Twins, Elara knew without knowing how.

And herself—older—sat nearby in a wide, throne-like chair, wrapped in warmth, a steaming drink cradled in her hands. She wasn't smiling widely. She didn't need to. Her expression held something steadier than happiness: peace. Certainty. The quiet satisfaction of someone watching the magic she loved being made by others she trusted.

Then Ava laughed too loudly, too close, and the vision slipped away like breath on glass.

Elara blinked, heart pounding, the familiar hearth before her unchanged, the snow still falling, the lantern standing cold and faithful by the window. She pressed her fingers briefly to her chest, unsettled but not afraid.

Some wishes, she thought, didn't fade.

They waited.

A Light Not Meant for One Lifetime

The air had that particular stillness that came after a night done correctly: faint ash on the tongue, pine lingering in the beams, the low, patient warmth of embers that hadn't been allowed to die. Pale winter light seeped in through the window in a thin line, too timid to call itself morning yet, and it cut across the floor like something cautious. Snow pressed close to the glass, softening the outside world into a blur of white and shadow, and for a moment Kael lay still and let his body catalog the aches.

His shoulders burned with the dull throb of yesterday's woodpile. His hands felt bruised along the knuckles where cold had bitten through wool and stubbornness. His calves ached from standing too long, too still, keeping watch in a way that had never been asked of him but had always been expected all the same. He had not slept. Not truly. He had drifted in fragments—eyes closing, mind snapping awake again at the slightest shift in the house—until the line between rest and vigilance had blurred into something that was neither. He could still feel the night in his bones, like cold tucked beneath the skin.

He sat up slowly, breath shallow, and listened.

Above him, in the loft, Mayli breathed.

It was the first sound he reached for every morning—soft, even, untroubled. The night had not taken her joy. The house had not stolen it in her sleep. Her breathing was the same as it had been when she was tucked into her blankets, the same as it had been when she'd sighed in her dreams and curled tighter without waking. Kael kept his eyes closed for a heartbeat longer than necessary, holding that proof in place as if the world might change its mind if he looked too quickly.

When he finally rose, he did it quietly, the way he always did, feet finding the places on the floorboards that complained the least. He moved through the room with the practiced care of someone who understood how easily sound became accusation. The lantern stood by the window, glass dark now, wick spent, having done exactly what it was meant to do. Kael picked it up, trimmed the wick, and wiped the rim with a cloth until soot no longer smudged his fingertips. He didn't do it because anyone had asked him to. He did it because leaving it undone felt like leaving a door unlatched.

The hearth was banked low, embers glowing faintly beneath a crust of ash. He stirred them gently, coaxing them back into breath, not enough to flare the fire and waste wood, only enough to ensure it would warm the house when the others woke. He fed it two small splits of pine, listening for the soft crackle that meant the flame had caught, then adjusted the log so it would burn evenly instead of collapsing in on itself. The sound of the fire was small, obedient. Kael envied it, briefly and without bitterness.

Outside, the world remained blank. Snow filled in every shape, rounded every edge, erased every trace of the work that had been done the night before. It would look untouched to anyone who opened the door and glanced out. As though the farm kept itself. As though the animals had secured their own latches. As though the lantern had lit itself and held

52

through the night out of pure devotion to tradition. Kael watched the white beyond the glass and felt something familiar settle in him: the quiet understanding that the world often preferred its magic without witnesses.

He crossed the room and paused beneath the loft ladder, head tilted slightly. Mayli's breathing shifted—one soft sigh, a small murmur that might have been a word in a dream—and Kael held still until the sound smoothed again. He did not climb up. He didn't need to. He didn't want to be seen hovering. He simply stayed where he was, attentive and out of the way, letting the morning arrive at its own pace.

His parents' door remained closed. Of course it did. They slept well on Lumenfall. They always had. Something in them relaxed when everything was in order, when the right light had burned, when the rules had been followed without their having to watch it happen. Kael had never heard them say thank you for that ease. He had never expected it. Gratitude was for gifts. What he did was not considered a gift. It was considered the way things were meant to be.

He rinsed his hands at the basin, water cold enough to sting, and the sting kept him sharp. The sky lightened by degrees, not brightening so much as giving up on being night. Gray bled into pale blue. The snow reflected it faintly, turning the world outside the window into something soft and unreal.

Kael found himself looking toward the hearth without meaning to, eyes tracing the line beneath the lantern where the gifts had been placed. He had left Mayli's there in the night, positioned exactly where her gaze would fall, adjusted twice, then once more, until it felt right. He could still remember the way his pulse had climbed when he slid it into place, the strange tightness in his throat that had nothing to do with cold. He had prayed, too—quietly, almost reflexively—asking Mēnô to keep her asleep, to keep the night from noticing her, to keep the magic intact long enough to be found in the morning.

It had worked.

Kael didn't smile at that. He didn't allow himself to. Satisfaction could soften you if you let it. But he felt it anyway, low and steady, like embers refusing to die.

A creak sounded above him—lighter than the house settling, sharper than a dream-shift—and Kael's attention snapped upward instantly. Mayli moved again, blankets rustling. A small foot found the ladder rung. Kael stepped back without thinking, the motion smooth and immediate. Not hiding exactly. Just… making space. Making sure she would have the moment without his shadow in it.

The ladder squeaked softly as she began her descent, and Kael held his breath—not because he was afraid she would fall, but because there was something sacred about the first seconds of Lumenfall morning, the way belief sat bright and untested in a child's eyes. He didn't want to disturb it with reality.

Mayli's head appeared above the loft edge, hair tumbling loose around her face, cheeks flushed with sleep. She blinked down into the room, eyes still soft, and then her gaze snagged on the hearth.

She froze.

Kael watched her expression change in slow, dawning increments: confusion first, then recognition, then that bright widening of wonder that made his chest tighten painfully. Her mouth parted as if she'd forgotten how to breathe properly.

54

"Oh," she breathed, barely louder than the fire.

Kael stayed very still.

Mayli climbed down the ladder too quickly, nearly missing the last rung in her excitement, and then she was padding across the floor, hands clenched in her nightshirt as she approached the lantern like it might vanish if she moved too fast. The room held itself around her, waiting.

Kael felt the morning settle fully into place.

And for one quiet moment, before anyone else woke and the world returned to its ordinary shape, he let himself believe that this—this single breath of wonder—was worth every night he'd ever spent awake.

Mayli knelt before the hearth as though it were an altar, careful in a way she rarely was, her small hands hovering for a heartbeat before touching anything at all. Kael watched from the edge of the room, weight settled evenly through his feet, every instinct telling him to remain exactly where he was— present enough to intervene if something went wrong, distant enough not to intrude. This was her moment. He had made it so. He would not take it back by stepping into the light.

"They came," Mayli whispered again, softer this time, as if repeating it too loudly might undo it.

The door to his parents' room opened behind her, hinges giving a quiet sigh. His mother stepped out first, hair already smoothed, robe tied neatly as though Lumenfall mornings demanded no softness from her. His father followed, broader, slower, already surveying the room with the calm assurance of a man who expected things to be in order and found them so. Kael felt the familiar tightening between his shoulders—not fear, not quite—

but readiness, the reflexive preparation to be corrected if something was out of place.

Nothing was.

His mother's face softened the instant she saw Mayli kneeling there, the sharpness of her gaze easing into warmth. She crossed the room and rested a hand on Mayli's shoulder, grounding and possessive. "Of course they did," she said, voice low and pleased. "You were very good."

Mayli turned her head, eyes shining, as if the words confirmed something she had already known but needed to hear aloud. She reached for the gift slowly, reverently, peeling back the cloth with care that bordered on ceremony. Kael tracked every movement without meaning to—the way her fingers trembled just slightly, the way she paused before fully revealing it, savoring the anticipation like something sweet held on the tongue.

When she saw it, her breath caught.

Not in a burst of laughter, not in the sharp delight of surprise, but in a quiet, settling way, as though something had clicked neatly into place inside her. She lifted the carving and turned it in her hands, tracing its shape, testing its weight. Kael knew exactly what she was doing; he had done the same thing when he'd finished it, turning it over and over, making sure it felt right, making sure it belonged.

"It's perfect," Mayli said, not loudly, not for praise. Simply stating a fact. "They knew."

His father nodded, satisfied in the way he always was when a thing had gone according to expectation. "The Lumenkin always do."

Kael remained silent.

Breakfast followed, the house easing back into its usual rhythms with the addition of warmth and sound. His mother poured milk, tore bread rather than slicing it, moved with the calm efficiency of someone whose work had already been validated by the night. His father spoke of the weather, of the animals, of what would need doing once the day properly began. All of it ordinary. All of it untouched by the quiet miracle that had already happened.

Mayli spoke the most, words tumbling over one another as she speculated about the Lumenkin—where they might have come from, whether they'd been cold, whether they had seen the goats or the snow piled high along the fence. Her parents indulged her gently, redirecting when the stories grew too fanciful, smiling in that patient way that suggested they believed in tradition, not in magic.

Kael listened and ate.

He did not rush his meal, but he did not linger either. Hunger was a thing he understood how to manage. He chewed carefully, swallowed methodically, and let the warmth settle into him without comment. Across the table, Mayli cradled her gift close even as she ate, one hand never leaving it, as if afraid it might vanish the moment she looked away. Kael watched that too, the quiet possessiveness of a child who believed something had been chosen just for her.

No one thanked him.

No one looked at him at all.

That was not new. Kael had learned early how to live without acknowledgment, how to find completion in the work itself rather than in the response to it. Still, there was a particular kind of absence on mornings like this—a space where recognition *could* have lived and didn't. He felt it distantly, like pressure behind the eyes, and let it pass.

His mother stood and began clearing the table, movements brisk now that the moment had been enjoyed. His father discussed plans aloud, assigning tasks without looking directly at him, the assumption of Kael's compliance built so deeply into the fabric of the house that it no longer required confirmation. Kael nodded where appropriate, filed the instructions away, and waited for the natural pause that would allow him to leave without disrupting the shape of things.

It came quickly.

He rose, tied his cloak, and moved toward the door. No one stopped him. Mayli glanced up briefly, distracted, smile still bright, and lifted her gift slightly as if in farewell. Kael returned the gesture with a small nod she likely didn't notice.

Outside, the cold struck immediately, clean and honest. The door closed behind him with a soft finality, and the sounds of the house dulled at once, replaced by the wide, open quiet of morning. Snow stretched unbroken across the yard, fence lines softened, paths erased. Even his footprints from the night before were gone, filled in and smoothed over until the land looked untouched, as though he had never crossed it at all.

Kael paused on the threshold and looked back once, just long enough to confirm that the window still glowed faintly with reflected light, that the hearth still burned, that the world inside remained warm and complete without him.

That, too, was familiar.

He stepped forward into the snow, boots sinking with a soft crunch, and let the cold take him fully. Whatever satisfaction he felt at Mayli's joy settled low and steady inside him, not bright enough to be hope, not fragile enough to be disappointment.

The snow swallowed sound almost immediately, muting the house behind him until even the suggestion of warmth felt imagined rather than real. His boots broke the surface with a dull, steady crunch that marked his progress in a way nothing else did, each step briefly visible before the falling snow softened it again. The fence line passed to his left, posts hunched beneath white caps, wire buried and useless now, and beyond it the land opened wide and unclaimed, fields stretching outward until the horizon dissolved into sky.

He walked without hurry.

There was no one waiting for him out here. No task assigned. No correction poised on the edge of a voice. The day would find its shape later, when his father decided what needed doing, when the animals demanded their second round of care, when usefulness reclaimed him the way it always did. For now, the space belonged to him alone, and Kael let the distance grow between himself and the house without resisting it.

Cold crept deeper as he moved, settling into the seams of his clothing, pressing against his chest with familiar insistence. He welcomed it. Cold was honest. It did not pretend to be anything other than what it was. It did not soften for children or harden for those it disliked. It simply existed, impartial and unyielding, and Kael had learned how to live within its rules.

He followed no path. There was no need. The snow had erased them all, leaving the land smooth and undecided, and Kael took advantage of that, angling away from the road and the worn lines of habit toward the open center of the field. With each step, the farm receded further behind him, the low shapes of buildings shrinking until they were little more than dark smudges against the white.

He did not think of Mayli as he walked.

That surprised him, briefly. She had occupied so much of his attention through the night and the morning that he had expected her to linger, her delight echoing in his chest. Instead, the image of her knelt by the hearth felt complete, finished in a way that did not require revisiting. The magic had landed. It would carry itself now. Kael trusted that.

What remained was the quiet.

It pressed in gradually, not as absence but as presence, the kind of silence that made thoughts louder rather than swallowing them. Kael felt it settle around him, felt the way the world seemed to widen and narrow at the same time, the field stretching endlessly outward even as his focus drew inward, pulled toward a center he did not yet name.

He thought, then, of other Lumenfalls.

Not in detail. He did not catalogue memories the way some people did, arranging them into neat lines that could be revisited for comfort or regret. His past existed as a pattern rather than a sequence—work, watchfulness, quiet satisfaction followed by disappearance. He had always stepped out of the way once the morning arrived. He had always been the one who moved on while others stayed.

At first, when he had been smaller, he had wondered if that would change.

He remembered standing in doorways, lingering a moment too long, waiting for someone to notice him and say his name with something like warmth. He remembered learning, slowly and without drama, that such moments did not come unless they were summoned by necessity. He had adjusted accordingly. Adaptation was not bitterness. It was survival.

The field sloped gently downward, the snow deeper here where the wind had piled it high, and Kael leaned into the incline without thinking, legs burning faintly as he pressed on. His breath fogged thick and steady, a rhythm he could match his thoughts to if he wanted. He did not hurry it. There was no advantage in reaching the end of the field quickly. The end of the field would still be there when he arrived.

Somewhere above him, the sky brightened by a fraction, gray thinning toward pale blue, though the sun remained hidden. Kael squinted against the light reflexively, the glare off the snow sharp enough to sting. He pulled his cloak closer and kept walking, letting the cold settle deeper, letting the ache in his muscles ground him in the present.

This was the place he always came to when the house felt too full of other people's certainty.

Here, there were no expectations pressing down on him, no roles to perform beyond existing. The land did not care whether he was wanted or merely tolerated. It did not measure his worth in neat categories or weigh his presence against the inconvenience of his birth. It simply held him, vast and indifferent, and Kael found a strange comfort in that.

He slowed eventually, then stopped altogether.

The world around him stretched wide and still, the snow unbroken in every direction, the silence so complete it felt almost fragile. Kael stood there, hands hanging loosely at his sides, breath coming slower now, and felt the shape of himself in the open air. Fourteen years old. Too old to believe in stories meant for children. Too young to pretend he did not still want something unnamed and just out of reach.

He did not intend to pray.

That, too, surprised him when he realized it. Prayer had never been a habit of his, not in the way it was for others. He knew the names of the gods. He knew the stories. He understood the etiquette of asking. But prayer implied expectation, and expectation implied disappointment. Kael preferred to work within what he could see and touch.

Still, the thought crept in, unbidden.

If there is more than this.

He frowned slightly, as if the idea itself had spoken out of turn. More than this implied dissatisfaction, and Kael did not consider himself dissatisfied. He had food. He had shelter. He had purpose, even if it was not chosen freely. He had kept his sister safe through another Lumenfall night. Those were facts. Facts were enough.

And yet.

The quiet pressed closer, the field holding him in a way that felt suddenly deliberate rather than accidental. Kael became aware of his own stillness, of the way the world seemed to pause with him rather than move past him. Even the wind had stilled, the air hanging heavy and expectant against his skin.

His pulse quickened, a low thrum in his ears.

Kael lifted his head slowly, gaze sweeping the horizon, searching for some rational explanation—an oncoming storm, a shift in weather, anything that would restore the familiar balance of cause and effect. He found nothing. The field remained empty. The sky remained pale. The snow lay smooth and undisturbed.

He swallowed.

The distance he had put between himself and the house now felt less like escape and more like preparation, as though the land itself had drawn him out here for a reason he had not yet been told. The realization settled in him with quiet inevitability.

Whatever came next would not find him indoors.

Kael stood alone in the open field, breath fogging the cold air, and felt the edge of something pressing close—something that would not be ignored much longer.

It had weight now, a thickness that settled against his skin and threaded itself through his breath. The wind had stilled entirely, snowflakes hanging in the air longer than they should have before drifting down, as if the world itself were unsure whether it was permitted to continue. Kael did not move. He had learned early that when something large loomed close, stillness was often safer than resistance.

He did not kneel.

That had never felt right to him. Kneeling suggested submission, suggested that the one listening was owed something in return. Kael had nothing left he was willing to bargain with. Instead, he bowed his head just enough to acknowledge the moment, shoulders squared, feet planted firmly in the snow as though daring the ground to give way beneath him.

He kept the words inside.

Speaking aloud felt unnecessary, even dangerous, as if sound might fracture whatever fragile balance had settled around him. He folded the prayer inward instead, shaping it carefully, the way he shaped everything else that mattered.

Let it get better.

The thought surfaced without embellishment, stripped of hope or vision. He did not imagine a future transformed, did not picture warmth replacing cold or voices speaking his name with affection. He meant it narrowly, practically. Let the work ease. Let the nights pass without incident. Let the days stop asking more of him than he could give.

Let Mayli be safe.

That part required no shaping at all. It arrived whole and heavy, unquestioned. Safety was not something Kael had ever associated with himself, but Mayli deserved it the way children deserved light and shelter, without condition. He pictured her from the morning—the way her eyes had widened, the careful way she had held her gift—and felt something tighten in his chest, sharp and immediate.

Let me be enough.

The thought startled him.

Kael frowned faintly, as though the idea had overstepped some invisible boundary. Enough for what? The question rose at once, reflexive and sharp. Enough to work. Enough to endure. Enough to stay out of the way. Those things had never required divine intervention.

But the thought lingered, insistent, refusing to be dismissed.

Enough to matter.

His breath hitched before he could stop it, a faint cloud of white vanishing almost as soon as it appeared. Wanting to matter felt dangerous— too close to wanting more, and wanting more was a habit he had broken with care over years of quiet practice. Still, the prayer had already taken shape. He did not know how to pull it back without pretending it had never been there at all.

He stood in silence after that, letting the words settle, letting the cold creep deeper into his boots until his toes burned dully. The field stretched ahead of him, blank and unmarred, the snow smooth as linen beneath the pale sky. It looked untouched, as though no one had ever crossed it, as though nothing had ever happened here.

Kael almost turned back.

Almost told himself this was foolish, that prayers were for people who expected answers. He had lived fourteen years without one. He could live the rest the same way. He shifted his weight, muscles tensing as he prepared to move—

And the name surfaced anyway.

Mēnô.

It came without reverence and without anger, worn smooth by years of half-belief and habit. Mēnô, Moon God. Keeper of cycles and endings. God of things that came and went without apology. Kael had never known what to expect from a god like that, only that the moon had always risen whether people prayed to it or not.

Ménó, he thought again, more deliberately this time. *If you hear things like this. If you listen at all.*

He did not promise anything in return. Promises were traps, and Kael had learned to avoid them. He did not ask for favor. He asked for allowance.

Let it get better, he repeated, and then—because the morning demanded honesty whether he wanted to give it or not—he added, *or let me survive what comes if it doesn't.*

The cold shifted.

Not sharply. Not dramatically. Just enough that the air felt different against his skin, as though something had passed close by without touching him. Kael stiffened instinctively, eyes lifting, scanning the field for movement. There was nothing there. No figure. No shape. Only snow and sky and the quiet persistence of cold.

Still, the silence had changed.

It pressed inward now, dense and expectant, the way the world felt just before a storm broke or a branch snapped under too much weight. The sound of the wind dulled further, as though muffled by distance that had not been there a moment before. Even Kael's breathing sounded wrong in his ears, too loud, too present.

His pulse quickened.

He did not feel afraid.

66

That, more than anything else, unsettled him.

Kael had known fear. He understood it well enough to recognize its absence. This was something else—a sensation of being held in place without restraint, of attention brushing past him like a hand hovering just short of contact. He felt seen. Not assessed. Not weighed. Simply noticed, as one noticed a thing that existed and therefore mattered.

Kael straightened slowly, shoulders squaring despite himself.

"If you're listening," he thought, irritation threading through the words like a spine, "you could answer."

He expected nothing.

That, too, was habit.

The snow did not stop falling. The sky did not crack open. No voice spoke his name.

The quiet did not break.

It deepened.

Kael became aware of it first as pressure—not on his ears, not on his skin, but somewhere behind his eyes, as if the world had leaned closer and forgotten to retreat. The snow still fell, slow and patient, but it no longer sounded the way snow should. Each flake seemed to drift with intention, its descent measured, deliberate, as though gravity itself had paused to consider its next move.

Kael did not move.

He had learned, early on, that when something unfamiliar took an interest in you, motion often invited consequences. He kept his feet planted, weight balanced, hands loose at his sides, breath slow despite the way his pulse hammered against his ribs. The field remained empty. The horizon did not waver. And yet—

The cold loosened its grip.

Not vanished. Not replaced. Simply... stepped back, as if acknowledging his presence for the first time and deciding to make room for it. Warmth brushed his skin—not heat, not comfort, but the memory of it, the way embers remembered fire long after the flame had gone. Kael's breath caught, shallow and sharp, and he swallowed hard, fighting the instinct to look down at his hands, to check whether he was still himself.

The snow beneath his boots changed.

It did not melt. It did not move. It simply ceased to feel like snow at all, the texture flattening beneath his feet into something solid and worn, as if countless lives had passed over it before him. Stone, warmed by long use. Ground that had been *kept*. Kael's heart stuttered, and before he could stop himself, he lifted his gaze.

The field was gone.

A hearth burned before him.

It was larger than any he had known, wide and deep, firelight rolling rich and steady across carved stone and dark wood. Greenery draped the mantle—winter-bright leaves threaded with pale lights that pulsed softly, alive in a way no decoration had any right to be. The warmth reached him fully now, settling into his bones, easing aches he had never admitted to carrying.

68

Children laughed.

The sound cut through him clean and sharp, bright as struck glass. Two of them—twins, though the certainty arrived without explanation—ran in looping, chaotic patterns around the hearth, their movements mirroring and clashing all at once. Their laughter filled the space, fearless and unrestrained, the kind that assumed the world would catch them if they fell.

A man stood nearby, laughing with them.

He was tall, broad-shouldered, his medium blond hair catching the firelight until it gleamed almost metallic. Power radiated from him—not loud, not showy, but undeniable, the kind that bent the space around him without asking permission. The children darted in and out of his reach, tugging at his sleeves, clambering against him without hesitation, and he caught them easily, spinning them once before setting them back on their feet. Kael felt the weight of that power instinctively and knew, without knowing how, that it could burn worlds to ash if it chose.

And it chose not to.

Across the room, seated just beyond the reach of the fire's heat, was a woman.

She sat in a wide, high-backed chair that was less throne than anchor, carved and worn by years of use. A warm drink steamed gently in her hands, cradled without urgency, and her posture was relaxed in the way only people who belonged somewhere ever truly were. Her hair fell in a wild cascade of deep red curls, untamed and unmistakable, catching the firelight as if it had been made for it. She watched the children with a calm that did not waver, her gaze steady, knowing.

Her eyes lifted.

They met Kael's.

The recognition hit him like a physical blow.

Not surprise. Not curiosity.

Acceptance.

She did not ask who he was. She did not question why he stood there, half-frozen between worlds. She looked at him the way one looked at something expected finally arriving—not relieved, not triumphant, but certain. As if his presence completed a shape she had always known was incomplete without him.

Kael's breath stuttered.

He did not know her name.
He did not know her story.
He did not know how he had come to stand in a place that felt more real than anything he had ever touched.

But he knew—deep, bone-deep—that he was wanted there.

Not useful.
Not tolerated.
Wanted.

The realization was so foreign it hurt.

He became aware of himself then, truly aware, in a way he never allowed. He stood taller here. Older. Scarred in ways he had not yet earned, power coiled beneath his skin like a second pulse. He was not small. He was not out of place. The space around him accommodated his presence without protest, without the subtle resistance he had grown accustomed to pushing through.

The woman's gaze softened—not pitying, not indulgent, but resolute. She knew something he did not. That knowledge sat between them, heavy and unspoken, and Kael understood without being told that she would not offer it freely. Some things had to be lived.

The warmth deepened.

And with it came pain.

It arrived not as images, not as scenes, but as weight—blood on stone, fire in the sky, loss layered upon loss until even victory tasted of ash. Kael felt it press against his chest, the cost of what he was seeing, the inevitability of it. This future was not a gift. It was a *reckoning*.

He would bleed for it.
He would lose for it.
He would be alone for long stretches of it.

And still—

The laughter rang out again.
The fire held steady.
The woman did not look away.

Kael understood, with a clarity that frightened him, that the wanting he felt here would be earned only through suffering. That whatever path led to this hearth would take everything he was and demand more besides.

The vision began to thin.

The warmth receded first, followed by the sound of laughter, then the fire itself dimming until it was nothing more than a memory of light behind his eyes. The woman held his gaze until the last possible moment, her expression unchanging, as if imprinting herself into him by force of will alone.

Then she was gone.

The field rushed back in around him—snow, sky, cold biting sharp and immediate. Kael staggered, boots sinking into drifts that felt suddenly too real, too heavy. His hands shook, breath tearing from his chest in short, uneven pulls as the world resumed its ordinary indifference.

He bent forward, bracing his hands on his knees, heart pounding.

Nothing had changed.

And everything had.

Kael straightened slowly, eyes burning, and stared out across the empty field.

He did not know when.
He did not know how.
He did not know who the gods thought they were, showing him such a thing.

But he knew this:

Whatever waited for him would hurt.

And he would walk toward it anyway.

Under the Moon

The moon village revealed itself the way secrets did—gradually, and then all at once.

Hima had been watching the path beneath his feet, tracing the pale stone with his eyes as it curved through the trees, when the forest thinned and the land seemed to open its hands. The village rose from the earth rather than sitting upon it, pale stone shaped into rounded dwellings that curved inward, roofs dusted with snow that clung as if it belonged there. Lanterns lined the paths and clustered in the square beyond, their glow cool and silvered, not firelight so much as moonlight given shape. The air felt different here— quieter, thicker, as though sound itself had learned to move carefully.

Hima slowed without meaning to, his steps instinctively matching the pace of the place. He felt Amalthea's hand tighten around his, warm and sure, and when he glanced up she smiled down at him, her expression soft with recognition. One of her tails brushed his back, a familiar, grounding pressure, and the faint tension he hadn't known he was holding eased at once.

"We're here," she said, gently, as if the village might overhear anything louder.

They were not alone.

Moon elves emerged from doorways and side paths, drawn not by announcement but by awareness, their movements unhurried and precise. Cloaks edged with frost-thread caught the lantern light, eyes reflecting silver on silver as gazes lifted toward the newcomers. The moment they saw who walked with Hima—who walked *ahead* of him—the village shifted. Conversations quieted. Bodies angled subtly inward. Heads bowed, some deeply, others only by instinct, like grass bending beneath a passing wind.

Hima straightened.

He always did when Father entered a space.

Mēnô moved through the village without breaking stride, his presence sharpening the night around him. The moon overhead seemed brighter where it hovered above his path, its light drawn taut and clean, shadows crisp at his feet. Hima had learned, without ever being told, that this was how the world responded to Father. Space made room. Sound softened. Order settled.

Amalthea changed the village in a different way.

She stepped forward into the square and released Hima's hand, her near-human form blurring just enough that her **seven tails** unfurled behind her, long and graceful, moving with lazy independence. They brushed the snow without leaving tracks, caught the lantern glow and reflected it back brighter, warmer. A soft sound rippled through the gathered villagers—not fear, not surprise, but something closer to relief.

Children stared openly.

Hima watched as two small moon elf children edged closer, their curiosity outweighing their caution. Amalthea noticed immediately, her attention instinctive and kind. She knelt, lowering herself to their height, and one tail curved forward in a slow, deliberate offering.

The children hesitated, then laughed when Amalthea's smile turned playful. "Go on," she said lightly. "They won't bite unless I ask them to."

Fingers brushed fur, tentative at first, then more confident, and Amalthea's tails flicked in response, alive and responsive. The children's delight was immediate and unguarded, faces lighting as if they had been granted something sacred.

Hima watched, absorbing the scene without question.

Mum had seven tails.
Seven meant old.
Old meant wise.

It meant she understood the world in ways others did not.

The village elder approached, her steps careful, her head bowing deeply toward Mēnô before she turned to Amalthea with a smile that held both reverence and affection. "You honor us with your presence on Lumenfall," she said, voice steady and sincere.

Mēnô inclined his head. It was not quite a bow, but the elder accepted it as one, relief flickering briefly across her face.

Lanterns multiplied as the night settled fully, strung between buildings and clustered around the wide, low hearth at the center of the square. The scent of snow mingled with resin and something sweet simmering somewhere nearby—candied roots or moon-fruit, Hima guessed, the smell threading warmth through the cold air. Voices rose and fell softly, respectful without being hushed, as though Lumenfall itself asked people to be gentle with their joy.

"Is this where the gifts happen?" Hima asked quietly, tugging at Amalthea's sleeve.

She looked down at him, amber eyes catching the lantern light until they glowed. "Partly," she said. "Lumenfall looks different everywhere. That's how you know it's real."

He nodded at once. The answer satisfied him completely.

A group of elders arranged offerings near the hearth—small bowls, carved tokens, evergreen sprigs placed with careful hands. Children gathered at the edges of the square, excitement held just barely in check, glancing between the adults and the moon overhead as if waiting for permission from the sky itself.

Hima felt eyes on him again—not unkind, but curious, measuring. He stepped closer to his father, not touching him, simply aligning himself with that gravity. The villagers noticed. Some smiled. Others bowed again, just slightly, acknowledging the shape of something they sensed but did not name.

Amalthea's tails shifted behind him, one brushing his shoulder in a brief, reassuring touch. "You're doing well," she murmured, meant only for him.

Pride bloomed warm and immediate in his chest.

The moon climbed higher, flooding the square with silver light, and a hush fell—not commanded, not enforced, but shared. The village drew inward toward the hearth, toward the night, toward the balance Lumenfall promised.

Hima looked from the people to his parents, from Amalthea's warmth to Mēnô's stillness, and felt the shape of the world settle into him.

Once the first stillness broke, the village began to breathe again.

It happened subtly, like frost melting under steady light rather than sudden heat. Conversations resumed in low tones, bodies loosening from their instinctive alignment around Mēnô, movement returning to the square in careful increments. Amalthea seemed to sense the shift without looking for it. She rose smoothly from her crouch and moved among the villagers as though she had always belonged there, her seven tails drifting behind her in slow, unhurried arcs, each one catching light and attention in equal measure.

Where she passed, people softened.

Moon elf elders greeted her with nods and murmured welcomes, hands briefly brushing her sleeves in gestures that were equal parts reverence and familiarity. Younger villagers smiled openly, some offering small gifts—wrapped sprigs of evergreen, carved trinkets, bowls of sugared fruit—as though compelled to contribute something of themselves to her presence. Amalthea accepted each offering with grace, thanking them by name when she could, her voice warm and unhurried, never rushed even as the square filled around her.

Hima followed at her side, close enough that one of her tails occasionally curled back to brush his arm or shoulder, a quiet tether he had long since learned to rely on. He watched the way people reacted to her—the way shoulders eased, the way tension slid from faces that had been careful only moments before. Children drifted closer, emboldened now, eyes wide as they tracked the slow movement of her tails.

Amalthea noticed them all.

She knelt again, laughing softly as a cluster of children gathered around her, their voices bubbling with questions she answered patiently. One tail wrapped loosely around a child's waist to keep them from slipping on the snow; another flicked playfully when someone tugged too hard. Her laughter threaded through the square like warmth through stone, not loud, but persistent enough to change the temperature of the night.

Hima felt it keenly.

This, he understood, was another kind of power.

Not the kind that demanded space or stilled sound, but the kind that invited closeness, that drew people inward rather than pushing them back. He watched as villagers who had bowed stiffly to Mēnô now leaned toward Amalthea, seeking her attention without fear. She gave it freely, never hoarding it, never rationing her kindness as though it might run out.

An elder woman pressed a steaming cup into Amalthea's hands. Amalthea accepted it with a grateful smile and passed it to Hima without hesitation. "Careful," she murmured. "It's sweet."

He took it, both hands wrapped around the warmth, and sipped obediently. The liquid tasted of honey and herbs, rich and grounding, and Hima felt the cold ease in his chest. Amalthea rested a hand briefly at the back of his head as he drank, fingers gentle, familiar.

"Stay close," she said, not as a warning but as reassurance.

He nodded, pride flickering at being trusted rather than commanded.

Across the square, Mēnô stood apart, observing. He spoke when approached, his words measured and exact, his attention given sparingly but meaningfully. Villagers listened intently when he addressed them, heads

78

bowed, bodies angled toward him as though toward a fixed point of gravity. Hima noticed the difference without naming it: where Amalthea drew people in, Mēnô defined the edges of the space they occupied.

Both were necessary.

At least, that was what the village seemed to believe.

Lanterns were lit one by one, their glow reflecting off snow and stone alike, until the square shimmered with layered light. The hearth was prepared carefully, offerings arranged with deliberate symmetry. The air filled with quiet anticipation, a sense that something important was unfolding not because it had been declared, but because everyone had agreed to treat it as such.

Amalthea moved back toward Hima then, her attention returning fully to him. She brushed snow from his sleeve, straightened the collar of his cloak, her touch efficient but affectionate. "You're very quiet tonight," she observed, amusement softening the words.

"I'm watching," Hima replied, earnest.

She smiled, pleased. "Good. Watching teaches you more than speaking."

He accepted this immediately.

Around them, the village settled into its rhythm—children corralled gently by parents, elders murmuring final instructions, the hearth waiting patiently for flame. Amalthea's tails stilled slightly now, their movements slower, more deliberate, as though attuning themselves to the night's purpose. When she glanced toward Mēnô, there was understanding in her eyes, unspoken but firm.

Hima stood between them, cup empty and warming his hands nonetheless, and felt something settle into him with quiet certainty.

The world had room for warmth.
The world had room for law.
And tonight, at least, the two existed side by side without conflict.

Hima felt it first in the way the square seemed to tighten, not closing in but drawing its edges inward, like breath pulled deep into the lungs. The lantern light sharpened, shadows lengthening and growing more precise against the pale stone, and conversations softened further, voices lowering without anyone needing to ask. Even Amalthea's tails slowed, their lazy arcs stilled into a more deliberate grace, though they did not vanish. They never vanished for him.

Mēnô stepped forward.

He did not raise his voice. He did not lift a hand. He simply entered the center of the square, and the village aligned itself around him as naturally as tide to moon. Elders straightened. Children hushed. The hearth seemed to wait.

Hima felt his spine draw taut without conscious thought, his posture correcting itself the way it always did in his father's presence. He stood a little taller, feet placed more carefully beneath him, chin lifted just enough to be seen but not enough to challenge. This was not fear. It was attention. He had learned the difference early.

Mēnô's gaze swept the gathered villagers, assessing without haste, and where it lingered, people bowed more deeply, gratitude and reverence mingling in equal measure. When his eyes finally came to rest on Hima, the weight of that attention pressed warm and heavy against his chest.

80

"You have grown," Mēnô said.

It was not praise in the way Amalthea offered it, freely and often, but it was acknowledgment, and Hima felt it all the same. Pride flared bright and immediate, a sharp, satisfying warmth that cut through the cold far more effectively than the cup he still held.

"I try," Hima replied, careful and earnest.

Mēnô nodded once, slow and deliberate. A hand settled briefly on Hima's shoulder, firm and grounding, the touch measured as everything else about him was. "Trying is not enough," Mēnô said calmly. "But it is a beginning."

Hima absorbed this without hesitation.

Around them, the village listened as if the words had been meant for all of them, not just a child standing beneath the moon. Amalthea remained close, her presence a steady counterbalance at Hima's side, but she did not interrupt. She did not soften the statement. She trusted him to understand it in his own way.

The hearth was lit then, flame catching quickly, rising clean and bright. Its light reflected in Mēnô's eyes, silver and unblinking, and Hima watched the way the fire responded to him—steady, obedient, contained. There was comfort in that. Fire that knew its place did not burn villages down.

Mēnô spoke to the elders next, his words precise, outlining the order of the night, the placement of offerings, the timing of the gifts. There was no flourish to it, no indulgence in ceremony for ceremony's sake. Everything had purpose. Everything served balance. The elders nodded along, accepting each instruction without question.

Hima listened closely, committing the rhythm of it to memory.

This, he understood, was how the world stayed intact.

When a child near the edge of the square shifted too close to the hearth, Mēnô's gaze flicked toward them, sharp as moonlight on ice. The child froze instantly, chastened without a word being spoken, and stepped back. The moment passed, order restored.

Hima felt no discomfort watching it.

Correction was not cruelty. Correction prevented disaster. He had been taught that much already, even if no one had ever said it outright.

Amalthea knelt beside him again, one tail curling protectively around his back as the ceremony continued. Her hand brushed his sleeve, a quiet reminder of warmth and closeness, and Hima leaned into it without thinking. He did not feel pulled between them. He did not see a contradiction.

Mum brought comfort.
Father brought structure.

Both made the night work.

As the village settled fully into the rhythm of Lumenfall, Hima stood between them, firelight dancing across his face, and felt something important take root inside him. The world was not gentle by default. It had to be kept that way. Love helped, yes—but order made love possible.

He watched his father oversee the night with calm authority and felt a swell of certainty.

The fire settled into itself as the ceremony continued, flames steady and contained, their light casting long, deliberate shadows across the stone. The village moved in practiced harmony now, elders guiding children into place, offerings arranged with careful symmetry. Nothing was rushed. Nothing was left to chance. Hima watched it all with the quiet intensity he brought to anything he meant to understand.

It made sense to him.

The night worked because everyone knew what they were meant to do.

He stayed close to Amalthea's side, the curve of one tail still warm against his back, grounding him even as his attention followed his father's movements across the square. Mēnô spoke rarely now, but when he did, the village responded immediately—hands stilled, heads turned, the flow of the evening adjusting around his words without friction. Hima felt a small, private satisfaction in that, as though the smoothness of it reflected well on him too.

A group of younger children were gathered near the hearth, their excitement held just barely in check. One boy bounced on the balls of his feet, glancing repeatedly toward a basket of wrapped offerings set aside for later. An elder murmured a reminder to wait, and the boy stilled at once, cheeks flushed with effort.

Hima studied the exchange, brow furrowing slightly.

He tugged gently at Amalthea's sleeve. "Mum?"

She leaned down at once, attentive. "Yes, love?"

"What happens," he asked slowly, choosing his words with care, "if a child isn't good on Lumenfall?"

The question did not feel dangerous to him. It felt practical.

A hush rippled outward—not sudden, not sharp, but noticeable all the same. Conversations nearby softened further. A few elders glanced toward Mēnô, then back to Hima, their expressions unreadable. Amalthea did not tense, but one of her tails flicked once, thoughtful.

Mēnô turned.

He did not look displeased. If anything, his expression held something like approval—interest, perhaps, at being asked something that mattered. He approached without haste, the villagers parting easily to give him space. When he stopped before Hima, the firelight carved his features into silver and shadow.

"That depends," Mēnô said calmly, "on what you mean by good."

Hima considered this. "If they lie," he offered. "Or don't listen. Or hurt someone."

Mēnô nodded once, as though the list had met his expectations. "Then they are reminded," he said, evenly, "that actions have weight."

"Do they still get gifts?" Hima asked.

The question landed softly, but it landed.

Mēnô did not answer immediately. He let the pause stretch, long enough for Hima to feel it without discomfort, long enough for the village to lean subtly inward. "Gifts," Mēnô said at last, "are not rewards. They are acknowledgments. When order is kept, acknowledgment follows. When it is broken, correction comes instead."

Hima absorbed this, nodding slowly.

"What kind of correction?" he asked, not frightened—only curious.

"Cold," Mēnô replied, without hesitation. "Distance. Consequence. These things teach restraint. Restraint keeps the world from breaking."

The words were not sharp. They were not cruel. They were offered as fact, no different from explaining why fire burned or why the moon rose and fell as it did. Around them, villagers nodded subtly, agreement moving through the square like a shared breath.

Hima felt something settle into place inside him.

That made sense too.

Amalthea knelt beside him then, her movement smooth and unhurried. One of her tails wrapped gently around his shoulders, drawing him just a little closer. "Sometimes," she said softly, her voice warm but steady, "children need time instead. Not cold. Not fear. Just time to learn."

Mēnô looked at her.

For a moment, the space between them felt charged—not hostile, not tense, but alert. Then Mēnô inclined his head, just slightly, acknowledging the addition without retracting his own words. "Time has its place," he said. "But it must be given shape. Otherwise, it teaches nothing."

Amalthea smiled, unbothered. "We teach in different ways," she said lightly, and pressed a kiss to Hima's hair.

Hima leaned into it, content.

He did not feel torn. He did not feel confused. The answers fit together in his mind as neatly as the offerings arranged around the hearth. Warmth and cold. Love and law. Both necessary. Both right.

He looked back toward the fire, watching the flames hold steady within their bounds, and felt a quiet certainty take root.

The world was not gentle by nature.
Gentleness had to be protected.
And protection, sometimes, looked like restraint.

A Sunlit Home

Solari woke to light.

It spilled through the narrow windows in long, honey-colored bands, warming the stone floor before it ever reached his bed. The air smelled of crushed herbs and baked bread, of clean ash and sun-warmed wool, and for a moment he lay still beneath his blanket, listening to the soft sounds of the house waking around him. A kettle murmured near the hearth. Wood shifted and settled in the walls. Voices—low, familiar—moved together in an easy rhythm he had known for as long as he could remember.

He smiled before he even opened his eyes.

When he finally sat up, the light caught in his hair and turned it brighter, almost gold, and he squinted against it, laughing quietly at himself. Lumenfall decorations hung half-finished along the walls—sun-thread garlands braided with dried flowers, small charms cut from thin slices of wood and etched with careful symbols. One had fallen during the night and lay crooked on the floor. Solari scooped it up and set it back in place before pulling on his clothes.

The house was small, but it was full.

Aelwen stood at the table, sleeves rolled to her elbows, hands steady as she ground herbs with a stone pestle. Her movements were precise, practiced, each rotation measured as she worked the scent of rosemary and citrus into the air. Brisiel hovered near the hearth, coaxing bread from the oven with a towel and a quiet hum, her hair loose down her back, the firelight catching in it as she turned.

"You're awake," Aelwen said without looking up.

Solari grinned. "The sun came in my eyes."

"That tends to happen," Brisiel replied lightly. She crossed the room and pressed a kiss to the top of his head, warm and quick, before ruffling his hair. "Wash your hands. You can help."

He did at once, scrubbing his fingers with unnecessary enthusiasm before returning to the table. Aelwen passed him a bowl without asking, and he began stirring carefully, tongue caught between his teeth as he concentrated. He liked being useful. He liked knowing where things went, how they were made, why they worked.

"What's this for?" he asked.

"Burn salve," Aelwen said. "For hands and arms. Just in case."

"Because of Lumenfall?" Solari asked, eyes bright.

"Because of life, sometimes the sun can be as harsh as it is beautiful, Sun Drop." Brisiel corrected gently from the hearth and smiled when he laughed.

They worked around one another easily, passing tools without speaking, finishing each other's thoughts when they needed to. Solari

88

watched them as much as he helped—the way Brisiel would reach for a cloth just as Aelwen realized her hands were full, the way Aelwen adjusted the flame without breaking conversation. It felt like watching the sun trace the same path it always did—steady, reliable, inevitable.

Outside, the village was already stirring. Solari pressed his nose briefly to the window, breath fogging the glass as he watched neighbors string sun-filigree between buildings and hang lanterns along the path. Voices drifted up, cheerful and expectant.

"Will Genesis really come?" he asked, unable to keep the wonder out of his voice.

Aelwen paused, pestle resting against the bowl. She exchanged a glance with Brisiel—not wary, not fearful, just thoughtful.

"Sometimes," Brisiel said. "The Sun God passes through when the offerings please him."

"Does he like gifts?" Solari asked.

Aelwen smiled, small and private. "He likes order."

That seemed reasonable enough.

Solari returned to his bowl, stirring more carefully now, imagining what it must be like to see a god made of light. He wondered if Genesis burned to touch, if his voice sounded like fire, if he noticed children watching from doorways. He wondered if the Sun God could see *him*.

"Careful," Brisiel murmured, stepping close to steady the bowl when his stirring grew too enthusiastic. Her hand lingered at his wrist a moment longer than necessary, warm and reassuring.

"I am being careful," Solari insisted, though he slowed all the same.

They laughed softly, the sound folding into the warmth of the room. The bread was cut and buttered, steam rising as Solari tore into his piece with unrestrained joy. Crumbs scattered across the table. Aelwen brushed them away absently, already reaching for another task.

"You'll track flour everywhere," she chided, fond rather than sharp.

"I will not," Solari said, crumbs clinging to the corner of his mouth.

"You already have."

He wiped at his face, grinning, and felt Brisiel's hand smooth his hair again, affectionate and automatic. He leaned into it without thinking, the way he always did.

This was how mornings went.

This was how Lumenfall began.

Later, they would walk to the square together. Later, the lanterns would be lit and the offerings arranged. Later, the village would gather and speak of tradition and blessings and the Sun God's favor. Solari imagined himself standing between Aelwen and Brisiel, hands held tight, watching the sky for signs of gold and flame.

For now, the house held them.

The light climbed higher, warming the walls, catching in the sun-thread garlands until they glowed. Solari watched his mothers move through the room, through his life, and felt certain—utterly, unquestioningly certain—that the world was good because it allowed this to exist.

They stepped into the street together, the light following them out as if reluctant to let go.

Solari walked between Aelwen and Brisiel, hands brushing theirs as they moved, the familiar press of their presence steadying him as the village unfolded around them. Lumenfall had drawn people from their homes early this year. Sun-thread garlands stretched from roof to roof, catching the morning light and scattering it back in soft flares. Lanterns—still unlit—hung ready along the paths, their glass washed clean, their hooks newly set. The air carried the low murmur of voices layered with anticipation, the sound of a community preparing itself to be seen.

At first, it felt no different than any other year.

Neighbors greeted them as they passed, nods exchanged, a few quiet smiles offered. Brisiel returned each one warmly, touching shoulders, asking after children and gardens with easy familiarity. Aelwen inclined her head politely, her attention already cataloguing details Solari barely noticed—the way the garlands were tied, the placement of offerings set aside for later, the subtle shifts in posture as people realized who was walking by.

Solari noticed those.

He always noticed when people looked at his mothers a moment too long.

A woman near the well paused mid-sentence when she saw them, her hand tightening around the rope before she forced herself to continue. A pair of elders lowered their voices as Aelwen passed, their conversation folding in on itself until it became indistinct. A man who had once brought his injured son to their door nodded stiffly and looked away too quickly, as though eye contact might obligate him to something he no longer wished to owe.

Solari frowned, confusion pricking faintly at the edges of his excitement.

"Did I spill something?" he asked Brisiel in a whisper, glancing down at his tunic.

She smiled at him immediately, smoothing a hand over his shoulder. "No, sun drop. You're perfect."

Aelwen's mouth tightened—not in anger, not in fear, but in calculation. She placed a hand briefly at the small of Brisiel's back, a gesture so subtle Solari barely registered it, and angled them slightly toward the main square.

The closer they drew, the more pronounced the watching became.

It wasn't hostility. Not yet. It was attention—measured, assessing, the kind that lingered just long enough to make the skin prickle. Solari felt it brush past him like heat, uncomfortable in a way he couldn't quite name. He pressed closer to Brisiel's side without thinking, and she responded at once, her arm curving protectively around his shoulders.

"People are just busy," she said softly, more to herself than to him. "Lumenfall makes everyone strange."

That sounded right. Solari nodded and let the explanation settle.

In the square, preparations were well underway. Elders arranged offerings near the central platform—baskets of grain, jars of oil, woven sun-charms laid out with careful symmetry. A stack of firewood had been set aside nearby, neatly arranged, taller than Solari was. He paused to look at it, curiosity stirring.

"That's a lot of wood," he said.

"For the hearth," Aelwen replied smoothly.

He accepted that and moved on.

As they crossed the square, a hush rippled outward—not sudden, not complete, but enough that Solari noticed it. Conversations faltered, then resumed at lower volume. Faces turned toward them, then away again. Aelwen's pace never changed, her posture unyielding, her gaze forward. Brisiel kept smiling, greeting those who met her eyes, her warmth undimmed.

Solari felt something shift inside him, a faint unease threading through his anticipation.

"Will there be songs this year?" he asked, partly to fill the quiet.

"Of course," Brisiel said quickly. "There are always songs."

"And gifts?" he pressed.

"Yes," Aelwen said. "For those who have kept order."

The words landed strangely, though Solari couldn't have said why.

A group of children ran past them, laughing, and Solari watched them go with a pang of longing. He knew most of them by name. He had helped patch scraped knees, deliver remedies for coughs and burns. Today, they did not slow. They did not wave.

He told himself it was because they were excited.

By the time they reached the edge of the square, the watching had settled into something heavier, less curious and more intent. Solari felt it then, the quiet pressure of being measured, weighed against something invisible. He reached for Aelwen's hand this time, his small fingers curling around hers.

She squeezed back once, firm and reassuring.

"Stay close," she said quietly.

"I am," Solari replied, and meant it.

Above them, the sun climbed higher, its light sharpening as it rose, gilding the village in gold. Lantern glass gleamed. Sun-thread caught fire. Everything looked beautiful—too beautiful, suddenly, like a painting stretched tight over something that strained beneath it.

Solari lifted his face to the light, squinting, heart still full despite the strange tension curling at its edges.

By midday, the village no longer felt like a place Solari recognized.

The warmth was still there—sunlight pooling in the square, laughter rising and falling as people moved about their tasks—but it had thinned, stretched tight over something brittle. Elders gathered more frequently now, their conversations folding inward, heads bent close together as though the air itself might overhear them. The hearth at the center of the square had been cleared and reinforced, stone scrubbed clean, the stack of firewood beside it growing taller as more was added with careful intent.

Solari noticed that no one asked *why*.

He trailed behind Aelwen and Brisiel as they moved through the square, delivering small satchels of salve and bundles of dried herbs to those who still accepted them. Some villagers took the offerings with murmured

94

thanks, eyes flicking nervously toward the elders before meeting Aelwen's gaze again. Others hesitated, hands hovering, then shook their heads and stepped back as if burned.

"We won't need it," one woman said stiffly, her eyes already sliding away. "The Sun will judge."

Brisiel smiled anyway, gentle and unoffended, and pressed the satchel into another set of waiting hands. Aelwen said nothing, but Solari felt the shift in her beside him—the way her shoulders squared, the way her pace became deliberate rather than easy.

"Why are they being strange?" Solari asked quietly.

Brisiel brushed her thumb across his knuckles. "People like rules," she said. "They feel safer when they think someone else is in charge."

"Genesis?" Solari asked.

"Yes," Aelwen said, a beat too quickly. "Genesis."

The name passed easily between them, spoken often now, carried on the air like a promise and a warning all at once. Villagers spoke of his coming openly, voices bright with anticipation as they prepared the square, as they polished lantern glass and replaced sun-thread that had frayed. Children were ushered away from certain areas, redirected with firm but pleasant words. The hearth was no longer a place to gather near; it was something to look at from a distance.

Solari watched an elder draw a circle in chalk around the base of the hearth, the white line stark against stone.

"What's that for?" he asked.

"To keep things contained," the elder replied, not unkindly, but without looking at him.

Contained felt like a strange word for a holiday.

Aelwen's hand found the back of his neck then, fingers warm and steady. "Go help Brisiel," she murmured. "She'll need you."

He obeyed at once, though he glanced back at the hearth as he went, unease prickling faintly beneath his skin. Brisiel was arranging bundles of dried flowers near the edge of the square, humming softly as she worked, the tune familiar and comforting. Solari knelt beside her and began sorting stems by color, just as she'd taught him.

"You're very quiet," she observed, smiling down at him.

"I think they're doing it wrong," he said, frowning.

She paused, considering him. "Doing what wrong?"

"Lumenfall," Solari said. "It's supposed to be nice."

Brisiel's smile didn't fade, but something in her eyes shifted, sharpening with concern. She smoothed his hair back from his face, her touch lingering. "It still is," she said softly. "Sometimes people forget what nice looks like. That doesn't mean it's gone."

Solari nodded, reassured, and returned to his task.

Across the square, Aelwen stood with the elders now, her posture rigid, her voice low but firm. Solari couldn't hear what was being said, only catch fragments carried on the air—*necessary, balance, tradition, before*

Genesis arrives. Each word slid into the next, building something he couldn't quite see but felt pressing closer all the same.

The sun climbed higher, its light sharpening from gold to something harsher, more blinding. Lanterns were tested and retested, wicks trimmed, oil topped off. The firewood stack loomed beside the hearth, neatly arranged, untouched.

Solari felt the square tighten around him, the anticipation no longer joyful but expectant, hungry in a way that made his stomach twist.

He looked up at Brisiel. "When does Genesis come?"

She followed his gaze toward the sky. "Soon," she said.

Her hand found his again, fingers threading through his with quiet urgency.

The door had barely shut behind them before Brisiel kicked off her boots and nudged the table back into place with her foot, already talking about how she'd wrapped Solari's gift twice because he was terrible at guessing by shape alone. Aelwen set the basket down and began unpacking without hurry, the rhythm of the house reasserting itself with comforting familiarity. The stew was reheated, bread torn rather than sliced, and Solari climbed into his chair still talking, still smiling, his words tumbling over one another as he tried to explain why he thought Genesis would definitely arrive *after* sunset and not before.

"I think he waits," Solari declared seriously, mouth full. "So he can see who's been good all day."

Brisiel laughed, warm and unguarded, and flicked a crumb at him. "Is that so?"

"Yes," Solari said, nodding hard. "Because if he came too early, it wouldn't be fair."

Aelwen hummed thoughtfully as she ladled stew into their bowls. "Fairness does matter to gods," she said mildly. "Or so they claim."

Solari grinned, pleased to have been agreed with, and leaned back in his chair, kicking his feet lightly against the legs. The house smelled like food and sun-warmed stone, the tension of the square already fading into something manageable, something they could laugh away once the door was closed and the world was reduced to three bodies and a shared table.

The door burst inward with a fury that shattered the moment completely, splintering into jagged pieces across the floor as villagers stormed inside.

There was no shout. No warning. Just bodies and noise and the sound of wood breaking apart as the latch gave way. The room filled instantly—boots trampling splinters, cloaks brushing the walls, shadows leaping as lantern light spilled in behind them. Solari screamed, the sound tearing out of him before he could stop it, his chair tipping backward as hands reached for him.

Brisiel moved first.

She lunged, grabbing Solari around the middle and wrenching him free as someone else's fingers closed on his sleeve. "Run," she said sharply, already moving, already pulling him through the narrow passage toward the back of the house. Solari stumbled, his bowl shattering on the floor behind them, stew splashing up the wall as they fled.

Aelwen turned just long enough to snatch a pouch from the table—instinct, not plan—before following them, her expression hard and focused, fear pressed flat beneath action. "Don't stop," she ordered.

They ran.

The house that had always felt small and safe suddenly seemed endless, rooms blurring past as Brisiel dragged Solari through the sleeping space, toward the storage alcove, toward the narrow rear door that opened into the alley behind the house. Solari sobbed, breath coming too fast, his magic flickering instinctively beneath his skin like trapped sunlight, the air around him warming, brightening.

"Hide," Brisiel whispered urgently, shoving him toward the alcove. "No matter what you hear, don't come out."

He shook his head violently. "No—no, I don't want—"

Hands closed around Brisiel's arm.

She cried out as she was yanked backward, her grip breaking, Solari tumbling to the floor as the villagers surged into the back of the house. Aelwen slammed herself between them at once, her body a shield, her voice sharp and commanding even as someone struck her across the face.

"Leave him," she snarled.

Solari scrambled to his feet, panic overwhelming him as he watched his mothers dragged away, Brisiel twisting and fighting, Aelwen striking out with controlled precision even as ropes were forced around her wrists. Someone caught Solari by the collar this time, hauling him backward as he screamed their names, his voice cracking, the heat inside him flaring dangerously bright.

"Mama! Mama!"

Brisiel found his eyes across the chaos, her face bruised, her mouth bloodied—but her gaze fierce and unwavering. "Solari," she shouted over the noise. "Listen to me. Whatever happens—"

She was struck then, the words cut short, and Solari's scream ripped through the house, raw and animal.

They dragged his mothers out.

The house emptied as violently as it had filled, leaving shattered wood, overturned furniture, and the smell of stew cooling uselessly on the floor. Solari was hauled after them, sobbing, thrashing, the world reduced to motion and fear and the impossible certainty that the laughter from moments ago had been a lie.

Outside, the village waited.

And the fire had already been built.

They did not let them kneel.

The ropes were forced tight around Aelwen's wrists first, coarse and unforgiving, biting into skin as she twisted against them with controlled, furious strength. She struck one of the villagers square in the throat with her elbow before another caught her from behind, driving the breath from her lungs and shoving her forward. She staggered, caught herself, and lifted her head again, spine straight despite the hands forcing her onward.

Brisiel fought harder.

100

She kicked and clawed and screamed Solari's name until her voice shredded raw, her body twisting violently as two men tried to hold her steady. One slipped in the snow and she wrenched herself free long enough to stumble toward Solari, arms outstretched.

"Sol–!"

They dragged her back by the hair.

Solari screamed.

It tore out of him in a sound he didn't recognize as his own, high and broken and endless. He threw his weight forward, nails scraping uselessly against the stone as he was hauled back, his small body shaking violently in their grip.

"Let them go!" he sobbed. "Please–please–please–"

Aelwen heard him.

She twisted sharply despite the ropes, her gaze locking onto him with devastating focus. "Solari," she said, her voice cutting through the chaos like a blade. "Look at me, sun drop,"

He did, tears blinding him, chest heaving.

"You listen to me," she continued, every word precise, deliberate. "You do not look away. You remember this. You remember *us*."

Someone struck her across the face.

She reeled but did not fall.

Brisiel was crying openly now, her body shaking as she fought the hands binding her to the stake. "I'm here," she sobbed, frantic, as if saying it enough might make it true. "I'm here, baby. I'm right here."

They forced her back against the wood.

The stake loomed behind them—too tall, too deliberate, stacked and prepared long before tonight. The villagers moved with grim efficiency, tying rope around torsos, arms, waists, securing them as if they were livestock rather than people who had laughed and cooked and loved only hours ago.

Solari screamed until his throat burned.

"I don't want this," he cried. "I'll be good—I'll be good—I promise—"

Brisiel's head snapped up at that, her expression breaking completely. "No," she said fiercely. "No, Solari. Listen to me."

Her voice shook, but it did not waver.

"You were already good," she said. "You never had to earn us. Do you hear me? We would choose you as our son in every life time."

He shook violently, sobbing, trying to pull free as the hands restraining him tightened.

Aelwen fought the rope again, muscles straining, teeth bared as she wrenched against the binds with a growl of effort. The rope bit deeper. Blood welled. She hissed in pain but did not stop.

"You are light," she said to Solari, breathless but unbroken. "And light does not ask permission to exist."

The torch was brought forward.

The crackle of flame was deafening in the sudden hush, the sound impossibly loud against the ringing in Solari's ears. Heat washed over the square, oppressive and immediate, the air shimmering as the fire was lowered toward the stacked wood.

"No!" Solari shrieked.

He twisted violently, something tearing inside his chest, something *waking* in response to the unbearable wrongness of it. The world around him seemed to glow too bright, too sharp, the sunlight overhead intensifying until it hurt to look at.

The fire caught.

It raced upward with terrifying speed, hungry and eager, flames licking at cloth and skin, the heat slamming into Solari like a wall. Smoke poured upward, acrid and choking, and Brisiel screamed—not in pain, but in *rage*.

"I love you!" she shouted over the roar of the flames. "I love you— don't forget me—don't let them take that from you—"

Her voice broke into a sob as the fire surged higher.

Aelwen did not scream.

She clenched her jaw so hard Solari thought her teeth might shatter, her eyes never leaving his even as the heat distorted the air around her, even as the flames climbed. Her presence was iron, unyielding to the last.

"Live," she said simply.

Something inside Solari broke open.

Light detonated outward.

It burst from his chest in a blinding wave, a scream made of sun fire that tore through the square and sent villagers reeling back, shielding their eyes as the air itself warped and screamed in protest. The fire buckled, flames bending unnaturally inward as if pressed by an invisible force.

Solari didn't know he was doing it.

He only knew he wanted the fire to stop.

For a heartbeat—just one—it did.

The flames stilled, frozen mid-roar, the smoke hanging impossibly in the air.

And then the light *answered.*

Genesis arrived like the end of an argument.

The brilliance of him eclipsed everything, the square plunging into reverent silence as his presence crushed sound and motion alike. The fire died instantly, heat collapsing into ash beneath his will. Villagers fell to their knees as one, foreheads pressed to stone, breath held.

Genesis looked past the pyre.

He looked only at Solari.

"You are wasting power," Genesis said calmly.

He stepped forward and closed his hand around Solari's wrist, his grip iron-hard, inescapable. Solari sobbed, reaching toward the blackened stake, toward the empty space where his mothers had been moments ago.

"Please," he begged. "Please—I need them—"

Genesis did not look.

"They are gone," he said, without cruelty and without mercy. "You are not."

He turned, dragging Solari with him as the boy screamed himself hoarse.

Behind them, ash drifted down like snow as the village he had once loved, turned into scorched earth in an instant. A pillar of bright beautiful light slammed down from the sky above, incinerating anything that may have left an inkling that a village once stood; his mothers, the pyre, the elders, the buildings. Gone.

Yet Lumenfall burned on as the Sun God's grip tightened a hair too tight around Solari's wrist, silence coming over them both as light consumed them, warm and comforting as he arrived at his new home.

The Celestial Realm.

Like Lumenfall?

Want to read the rest of these character's stories?

Read the Companion Series:

Eclipsed
Entwined
Unbound (TBA)

The Cost of Dawn (Spring 2026)

9 781969 842061